A Dry Creek Mystery Thriller

Hidden Beneath the Lies

K. H. Andersen

Chapter 1

Lacy Krammer hadn't slept.

The drone of the engines had become a second pulse, low and relentless in her bones, matching the throb behind her eyes. She sat upright in Seat 22A, knees pressed against the tray table, arms folded tightly across her chest. Her in-flight meal—some indistinct blend of rice and chicken—sat untouched beside a half-finished cup of black coffee gone cold.

The overhead light flickered.

She stared out the window, past her reflection and out into the vast nothing of night and scattered cloud, the dark Atlantic slipping away beneath the plane's wing. Home was somewhere on the other side of that darkness. Home—and a funeral.

Lacy shifted, rolling her shoulder where tension had begun to knot beneath the fabric of her hoodie. Home for the burial of the man who had taught her how to hold a hammer, how to tell a truth from a lie, how to listen without speaking.

Grandpa George had never missed a day of her life until she left Dry Creek.

Now he was gone. And she was going back.

The seatbelt sign pinged on just before a lurch of turbulence rocked the plane. A startled breath caught in her throat as her coffee trembled and sloshed in its paper cup. She grabbed it reflexively, her fingers steady even as her heart thumped hard. Instinct.

She hadn't cried. Not at the news. Not when she'd packed. Not now. A soldier's reflex: file it, box it, keep moving.

Her fingers flexed around the cup.

"You okay, miss?" The flight attendant paused in the aisle, one hand braced on the seatback.

Lacy blinked up, startled. "Yeah. Fine."

The attendant gave her a quick nod and moved on. Lacy let out a breath.

She turned back to the window. The clouds were clearing now. She could see the first edge of dawn coloring the sky beyond the wing—rose-gold bleeding into slate.

Lacy swallowed.

She had departed from Frankfurt over ten hours ago. Two more hours until she landed in Atlanta, then a connecting flight to Chattanooga. Her aunt had promised to pick her up. There'd be just enough time for them to stop at the house, change, and go straight to the church.

Her reflection in the window looked unfamiliar in the half-light. Hollow eyes. Freckles dulled by fatigue. Her hair pulled back too tight.

You're not ready for this, something in her whispered.

But another voice, deeper and older, rose to meet it: *Doesn't matter. Go anyway.*

George's voice. She could still hear it.

She let her gaze drift back to the clouds, her mind beginning to slip.

Back to the office.

Back to the moment a day ago when her world had cracked

and the orders had changed.

The file in her hands was a no-name petty theft case, third offense, court-martial pending. Nothing unusual. She'd been halfway through a notes summary when the knock came—three soft taps at her open door. Lacy looked up to see Captain Elridge standing there, face unreadable.

"Sergeant Krammer," he said quietly. "Can you step into my office a moment?"

Her stomach tightened. She stood immediately, tucking the file under her arm.

Inside his office, the lights were dimmed against the afternoon glare and the blinds were half-closed. Her Captain gestured to the chair opposite his desk then rounded to his own side, lowering himself slowly—as if what he had to say might buckle his knees.

He slid a manila envelope across the desk toward her.

"I'm sorry to be the one to tell you this."

She didn't reach for the envelope.

"It's your grandfather," Elridge continued. "George Peterson. He passed away two nights ago. Local law enforcement has ruled it a suicide."

The word didn't register—not fully. It landed, dull and heavy, without shape or meaning.

Lacy stared at the envelope. Her hand moved toward it, automatic. Inside, she knew, would be the official notification, the standard forms.

"I've already cleared emergency leave with Personnel," Elridge added, his voice gentler now. "You're approved to depart tomorrow. Flights are being booked."

She nodded once. Still hadn't spoken.

"If you need more than a few days, let us know. You'll have

time to settle affairs."

Lacy stood. "Thank you, sir."

The words came from a place outside her body. She took the envelope and left the office. She didn't remember walking back to the barracks, didn't remember packing. Just flashes—the duffle bag yawning open with the smell of boot polish.

And George's voice, faint and steady in her memory: *Don't run from the hard things, Lacy. They're the ones that make you strong.*

The flight from Atlanta touched down in Tennessee with a screech of rubber and a jolt that snapped Lacy upright. Her hands were already gripping the armrests before she knew it.

The plane slowed. Her stomach didn't.

Outside, the tarmac glistened with morning damp, the clouds still low and gray. It was just after dawn, and the air on the jetway smelled like rain-soaked concrete and pine—scents she hadn't realized she'd missed until they hit her all at once.

As she waited at baggage claim, the bag she'd checked—a standard-issue duffel with her last name displayed across it in black block letters—came around the carousel.

Her bag collected, she then stepped through the sliding doors into the arrivals hall and saw her aunt waiting for her.

Margaret Peterson looked smaller than Lacy remembered. Her auburn hair had gone almost entirely gray, and her frame— once sturdy, like George's—now seemed thinner, the way grief thins people. She held a plain umbrella in one hand, a set of car keys in the other.

Their hug was brief. Firm, but not lingering.

"You made it," Margaret said softly. Her voice had always been calm, a librarian's voice.

"Yeah," Lacy said. "Just now. Flight was smooth."

A nod. "We should get going. The service starts at ten."

"Okay."

No talk of George. No *"how are you holding up?"* No *"I'm glad you're here."*

But Lacy didn't need those things. She was here. And that had to be enough—for both of them.

The pickup smelled like wet upholstery and gas station coffee. Margaret drove with both hands tight on the wheel, eyes fixed on the road ahead. The truck's heater rattled to life as they pulled onto the highway, humming low under the muted country station playing from the dash.

Lacy leaned her head against the cool window, watching as mist curled off the hills. The land looked the same—green and folded like a quilt, dotted with barns and rusted tractors. But it felt different too. Smaller somehow. More watchful.

They passed a row of mailboxes perched like birds on splintered posts. A faded billboard offered peaches and hand pies. Just ahead, the old "Welcome to Dry Creek – Monroe County" sign emerged through the fog, its paint chipped and surface bullet-pocked.

Lacy's chest tightened.

"That sign's been like that since I was ten," she said quietly.

Margaret gave a noncommittal sound. "They keep meaning to fix it."

Silence stretched.

Lacy glanced over. "You doing okay?"

Her aunt's mouth tightened. "It's been… a lot."

More silence.

Margaret cleared her throat. "We'll go straight to the house so you can change, then head to the church. There's a little time, but not much."

Lacy nodded.

The truck dipped and rose through the curves of the road. Familiar houses came and went—some with new siding, others sagging further into the earth. The land didn't care about grief. It just kept on being.

Margaret finally said, "Just be prepared. People mean well, but some don't know how to say the right thing."

Lacy gave a faint smile. "I'm used to that."

Margaret didn't smile back.

They rode in silence again. And this time, it felt like something was being held back. Not just grief. Something heavier. Unspoken.

Lacy didn't push. Not yet.

As they neared the farmhouse turnoff, a flicker of unease began to stir in her chest. As if the land itself remembered something she hadn't yet.

The truck crested a low hill—and there it was.

The farmhouse sat like a ghost at the end of the gravel drive, white paint worn thin on the boards, porch wrapped in fog. The same weathervane spun slowly above the barn roof, and the same sag in the porch made the swing tilt just a little to the left. It looked exactly as she remembered it. And at the same time, not at all.

Margaret turned onto the drive, tires crunching over wet stone as the truck slowed to a crawl.

George's truck still sat off to the side of the barn, backed into its usual spot, the tailgate down. As if he'd be out in a minute to load it with seed or firewood.

Lacy stared.

The porch light was on.

She didn't speak until they rolled to a stop.

"I'll just be a minute," she said, reaching for her bag.

Margaret nodded, not moving from the driver's seat. "I'll wait here."

Lacy climbed out, boots hitting the gravel with a thud that sounded too loud in the morning quiet. She stepped onto the porch, heart hammering, and pulled her house key from her pocket. The metal slid into the lock with a familiar click—a sound she hadn't realized she still remembered so clearly. She turned the knob and pushed the door open.

The scent hit her first: old wood, dust, faint smoke—and underneath it, something else. Time. The kind that settles into the floorboards when no one's home to stir it.

She crossed the threshold.

The house had been tidied, she could tell. Probably Margaret. But it hadn't been touched. Not really. George's boots were still by the door. His coat still hung on the hook, slightly askew like he'd thrown it up with one hand while juggling the mail in the other.

Her throat tightened.

She paused just inside the door, adjusted the strap of her duffel, then carried it with her toward the stairs. There would be no lingering in the entryway today. The chair by the woodstove was empty.

She moved quickly now—up the stairs two at a time. Her old room still had the faded quilt on the bed, the one George's mother had stitched by hand. Lacy dropped her bag beside it and unzipped it, pulling out a plain black dress she'd folded carefully between layers of uniform shirts and socks. She laid it across the bed for a moment.

She changed in silence, her movements automatic. Pulling her hair back. Wiping her face with cold water from the bathroom sink. She opened the small jewelry box on her dresser, fingers hesitating just a moment before lifting out the silver locket she hadn't worn in years. It had been a gift from George when she turned twelve—engraved with her initials on one side and a tiny compass etched on the other. "So you always know where home is, even if you're halfway around the world," he'd told her. She hadn't worn it since joining the Army. Now, it felt like armor. She fastened it around her neck.

Then she paused.

She was already halfway down the stairs when her eyes drifted to the china cabinet. Her fingers brushed the edge of it as she passed—polished wood, its secret compartment hidden just behind the middle drawer. George had shown it to her when she was nine, swearing her to secrecy. It had felt like being knighted.

She didn't open it.

Not yet.

Margaret's voice called softly from the porch, "Lacy?"

Lacy turned, gave the cabinet one last glance, and stepped outside.

Rain was beginning to fall. Light, cold, steady.

She locked the door behind her, but as she turned toward the truck, she felt it again—that flicker of knowing. Of something waiting.

Something the house hadn't yet said.

The rain picked up as they turned out of the drive, spattering the windshield with fast, deliberate taps. Lacy folded her hands in her lap, dress damp at the hem from brushing the porch steps. Margaret drove slowly, wipers struggling against the thickening drops.

Neither of them spoke.

Dry Creek unfolded around them—lush and overgrown, the way summer always left it. Ferns curled around mailbox posts, ditches ran full, and the mist blurred the lines between road and woods. It smelled like clay and pine needles and something faintly metallic, like a penny left out in the rain.

They rolled past a sagging fence line, its posts tilting under the weight of years, and Lacy pressed her fingertips against the window. The landscape looked worn and familiar yet distant—like a photograph left out too long in the sun.

Margaret cleared her throat, eyes still on the road. "You okay over there?"

Lacy blinked. "Yeah."

"You didn't have to come all this way. We could've postponed the service. Given you more time."

"No," Lacy said, a little too fast. "This is right."

Margaret nodded but didn't answer. The silence stretched again.

They passed the high school, the diner, the square with the rusted Civil War statue still standing guard over a patch of soggy lawn. Lacy glanced out at the storefronts—half of them shuttered, a few with new paint, but most exactly the same. She spotted the old Rexall sign above the pharmacy, its neon flickering weakly even in the daylight.

"Not much has changed," she said, more to herself than her aunt.

Margaret made a small sound in her throat. "Depends how you look at it."

It wasn't unkind, but something about the way she'd said it made Lacy glance sideways.

"What do you mean?"

Margaret kept her eyes on the road. "Just… people. They talk. They always did."

Lacy waited for more. But her aunt said nothing else.

As they passed the church—white clapboard, bell tower rising into the gray—Lacy saw the parking lot already filling. Pickup trucks, a few sedans, and a blue minivan she vaguely remembered from potlucks and school pickup lines. She felt her stomach tighten.

Margaret turned the steering wheel, gravel crunching as they pulled into the side lot.

"You can go in ahead of me," Lacy said, her hand already on the door handle.

Margaret didn't argue. "I'll see you inside."

The sky rumbled softly above them as Lacy stepped out, the rain now steady and insistent. She didn't run for cover.

She stood for a second alone in the lot, watching the people through the windows. Suits, black dresses, and umbrellas shaken off in the entryway.

She took a breath, then another, steadying herself.

And walked toward the door.

Inside, the air was heavy with damp coats and low whispers. Lacy slipped into the foyer, water beading on her sleeves, and felt the weight of eyes turning toward her. Conversations dimmed, then picked back up in softer tones. Recognition flickered across faces—some kind, some unreadable, a few edged with suspicion.

She moved toward the front where Margaret was already settling into a pew. The wooden floor creaked beneath her steps. Townsfolk on either side dipped their heads or offered polite, murmured condolences. None lingered.

Lacy scanned the room. The pastor stood near the pulpit, flipping pages in his worn Bible. A cluster of women arranged flowers near the altar, their hands quick and practiced. By the far wall, two men she remembered from the hardware store years ago leaned together, their voices low. But when her gaze brushed over them, they stopped talking.

Her stomach tightened again. The hush wasn't just grief—it was something else. Something guarded.

She slid into the pew beside Margaret, folding her hands in her lap. The wooden bench was hard beneath her, the hymnals stacked neatly in the pocket before her. She stared at the cross above the altar but felt only the echo of George's voice, steady and warm, urging her to stand tall.

The organ hummed to life. Lacy's throat closed. She watched as the sanctuary filled, more and more townsfolk slipping in, shaking rain from umbrellas, their faces marked not with sorrow but something tighter. Something that felt like fear.

When the doors creaked shut behind the last latecomer, she realized her hands were trembling. She curled them into fists in her lap and whispered to herself, *Just get through this.*

Chapter 2

The organ quieted to a thin, breathy hum, and the pastor stepped up to the pulpit with his Bible held like something fragile. Rain tapped the church roof in a steady, unhurried rhythm, and Lacy felt the damp in her sleeves where the water hadn't fully dried. The sanctuary lights gave everything a softened edge—the varnish on the pews, the brass of the cross, the lilies arranged in white domes that smelled faintly sweet and medicinal.

"This morning," the pastor began, voice low and even, "we remember George Peterson as a neighbor, a father, and a friend who gave more than he ever took." His eyes swept the room, pausing on Lacy only long enough to acknowledge her without pinning her in place. "He served this town with quiet dignity. He took great care with the small things that keep a community together."

He kept the records straight, Lacy thought. *He kept me straight.* She stared at the closed casket at the front—mahogany, a muted sheen, a spray of lilies and ferns draped across it. The lid had been shut before she'd arrived; the finality of it landed like a stone.

The pastor spoke of kindnesses that sounded both true and

too small: rides to doctors' appointments, a repaired porch step, a casserole delivered to a widow's door after a hard winter. "He listened more than he spoke," the pastor continued. "He gave people the gift of being heard."

Lacy's aunt sat very straight beside her, a folded tissue untouched in her hand. Margaret's profile was composed, lips pressed thin, gaze fixed on the cross as if it might give her instructions. Two pews back, Lacy's cousin Lucas kept his head down, jaw tight, and when she glanced over her shoulder, he looked away—quickly, as if burned.

A whispered current rustled the sanctuary and settled again. Lacy heard the smallest sounds too clearly: a child's shoe scuffing wood, the creak of a pew, someone stifling a cough. She tried to breathe evenly through the pressure in her chest.

Say he knew I loved him, she pleaded silently. *Say he wasn't alone.*

The pastor read a psalm about green pastures and still waters. It washed over her without sticking. Then he folded the ribbon into the Bible and closed it softly. "If anyone would like to share a memory, we invite you to do so—briefly." His eyes lifted. No one stood. A chair leg scraped and went still. The rain filled the space where words should have been.

Lacy felt the thought rise—*Stand up. Say something.* "Measure twice, cut once," George had told her on the porch one summer when she was nine, the hammer she held too big in her hand. *Slow is smooth. Smooth is fast.* She could almost smell the cedar shavings and lemon oil from his workbench.

But her knees wouldn't unlock. Her mouth stayed shut. The words she wanted to say—that he had been good, that he had believed in her when the world didn't—crowded her throat and went nowhere.

The pastor nodded gently, as if he'd expected the silence.

"Then let us pray." Heads bowed; Lacy's followed, though her eyes remained open. The prayer was simple, mercifully short: comfort for the grieving, rest for the departed, gratitude for a life well lived. When the congregation lifted the soft *amen*, the sound braided with the rain.

"In a moment," the pastor said, "the ushers will guide us row by row for final respects." He stepped down from the pulpit and laid a palm on the casket as if greeting an old friend. "Thank you all for your presence."

Lacy flexed her fingers, realizing she'd kept them clenched through the entire service. The tissue in Margaret's hand remained unused. The cousin behind them had already turned toward the aisle.

The organist found the first gentle notes of "Amazing Grace." The pew creaked as Lacy shifted her weight. Brief and solemn—that was all it was, and yet her heart pounded as if she were about to run.

Row by row, people began to rise.

The usher's hand brushed the pew, signaling their turn. Margaret stood first, smoothing her skirt with a practiced motion and her tissue still folded, still dry. Lacy followed, legs stiff, the weight of each step a little heavier than the last.

As she approached the casket, Lacy's breath hitched. She placed her fingertips lightly against the cool wood, the surface smooth and unyielding beneath her skin.

Her throat tightened. She bent her head slightly, lips close to the polished lid. "Goodbye, Grandpa," she whispered, so faint it barely reached her own ears. "I hope you knew. I hope you knew I loved you."

A memory swelled, unbidden. A summer storm when she was seven—lightning slicing the sky, thunder shaking the farmhouse walls. She'd hidden under the kitchen table, knees tucked to her chest and trembling at every crack of thunder. George had found her there, crouched low, and coaxed her out with steady hands. *Storms pass, Lacy. They always do. You just have to wait them out.* His voice had been calm, certain, a shelter stronger than the roof above them.

The echo of it steadied her now. Her fingers pressed more firmly against the casket before she finally let go.

Margaret's hand came to rest at her elbow, gentle but insistent. "Come on," her aunt murmured. The words carried both compassion and urgency, as if lingering too long would expose something raw.

Lacy stepped aside, allowing the line to move forward. Her cousin approached next, head still down, shoulders stiff. Others followed with murmured prayers and brief touches, their faces unreadable in the low light.

The sanctuary emptied slowly, each farewell clipped and quiet. Lacy held her place at the side aisle until Margaret gave her a pointed look toward the doors. She nodded, throat still tight, and let herself be ushered out with the rest.

Outside, the rain had deepened into a steady curtain, hissing against the church steps and pooling in the gravel lot. Vehicles pulled away one by one, tires splashing through puddles, taillights blurring in the gray. The pastor slipped out a side door with Lucas in tow, their figures quickly swallowed by the weather. Margaret gave Lacy a brief squeeze on the arm before hurrying toward the car. "I'll start the engine. Come when you're ready."

And then suddenly, there was no one.

Lacy stood at the entrance, the heavy wooden door closing behind her with a hollow thud. The silence between raindrops was immense, pressing in around her. Water trickled down her temple, darkening the edge of her black dress. She scanned the lot—emptying fast. Only a few umbrellas bobbed in the distance before vanishing into cars.

For the first time since stepping off the plane, she felt the full weight of it: George was gone, and she was standing on Tennessee soil without him. The church loomed at her back, familiar yet foreign, and every face that had turned toward her inside now seemed like a question without an answer.

She wrapped her arms around herself against the chill, her gaze caught between the fog-smeared hills beyond the cemetery and the closed doors behind her. A gust of wind rattled the bell tower overhead, and she thought of George again, steadying her in storms. Only now, the storm felt like it had just begun.

The scrape of shoes on wet gravel drew her attention. She turned her head sharply. A tall man approached with an umbrella tilted against the rain, his steps unhurried but direct. The black canopy glistened with rivulets, and when he got close enough, he angled it to shield her as well.

"Lacy Krammer?" His voice was warm but carried a thread of certainty, as though he already knew the answer. He held the umbrella steady, rain pattering on its fabric roof.

She hesitated, studying him. Mid-thirties maybe, dark hair damp at the edges, a face lined by wear more than age. His brown eyes were keen, assessing without apology. He wore a jacket that had seen better days and carried a leather notebook under one arm, its edges warped by use.

"Yes," she said carefully.

He offered a small nod, as though confirming a detail. "Marcus Bell. I'm a journalist. I cover local stories, community events. Obituaries sometimes, though I prefer the stories behind them."

Lacy stiffened, pulling her arms tighter around herself. "Now's not a good time."

"I understand." He reached into his jacket pocket, produced a plain business card, and held it out between two fingers. "I just wanted to offer my condolences. And—if you're ever willing—I'd like to talk about your grandfather. About the kind of man he was. People deserve to remember him right."

She took the card, more to end the gesture than accept the invitation. The cardstock was damp already, edges curling in her grip. Without answering, she slipped it into her dress pocket.

Marcus didn't press. Instead, he glanced toward the cemetery, his gaze thoughtful as though measuring the headstones against some hidden ledger. "Again, I'm sorry for your loss," he said quietly.

Then he stepped back, letting the umbrella shift until the rain was hers again. He walked toward the far end of the lot, scribbling something in his notebook even as water streaked the page.

Lacy watched him go, unease tightening in her chest. She hadn't spoken more than a handful of words, but she already felt exposed, like he'd read something on her face she hadn't meant to reveal.

She tucked the damp card deeper into her pocket as she moved toward Margaret's truck. The wipers squeaked back and forth when she opened the passenger door, warm air fogging the windshield from the heater already running. Margaret glanced at her but didn't ask questions, only shifted into gear as Lacy settled in.

As the truck pulled away, Lacy risked a glance through the rain-streaked glass. Marcus still stood there under his umbrella, notebook balanced in one hand and pen scratching across the page. His eyes lifted briefly toward the cemetery, scanning rows of headstones as though searching for more than dates carved in stone.

Lacy pressed her palm against her damp skirt, nerves prickling. What kind of journalist lingered at a graveside like it was an assignment? She tried to tell herself it was harmless— small-town curiosity, nothing more. But unease clung to her like the rainwater soaking into her shoes.

The truck's tires splashed through standing water, carrying them down the narrow road. Margaret gripped the wheel, her focus locked on the ribbon of asphalt. Lacy leaned her head against the cool window, watching Marcus shrink to a dark blur in the distance.

Her chest tightened. She wanted answers—about George, about why the town felt so hollowed out, about why her cousin wouldn't meet her eyes. But all she had was a stranger's card in her pocket and the certainty that someone was paying closer attention than they should be.

Back at the farmhouse, the gravel crunched under the tires as Margaret pulled the truck up the driveway. The rain had slowed to a mist, but Lacy's dress was still heavy with damp when she climbed out. Inside, the house smelled faintly of coffee, unchanged since morning. She slipped into her room and shut the door, eager to peel away the black dress and the weight it carried.

Chapter 3

Steam rose from the kettle as it clicked off, the sound sharp against the farmhouse's quiet. Margaret moved with a practiced gentleness in the kitchen, setting mugs on the counter, her shoulders a little stooped beneath the light. She didn't say much, only asking if Lacy preferred honey or sugar, her voice steady but hushed as if she were afraid to speak too loudly in George's absence.

Lacy sat at the old wooden table, fingers curled around themselves in her lap. The chair creaked when she shifted, familiar and strange all at once. She watched Margaret spoon loose tea into a ceramic pot, the motion precise and deliberate. It wasn't just tea she was tending; it was the silence between them, the cavern that had opened since the funeral.

"Drink something warm," Margaret murmured, sliding a mug toward her. "It helps, after a day like this."

"Thanks," Lacy said, her voice rasping. She wrapped her hands around the cup, letting the heat soak into her palms though her stomach twisted too tight to drink.

Margaret busied herself with tidying—folding a dish towel, straightening the salt and pepper shakers, adjusting a stack of unopened mail on the counter. Her hands always needed something to do. Each gesture was neat, controlled, but Lacy recognized the avoidance in it. Grief made some people talk, and others fidget. Margaret chose silence and order.

The clock over the stove ticked steadily, a sound that filled the space where conversation should have lived. Lacy wanted to ask—wanted to say, *"Do you believe it? That Grandpa would take his own life?"* But the words stuck in her throat. Margaret's posture warned her off: the slope of her shoulders, the way she kept her gaze fixed anywhere but on Lacy.

Lacy rubbed her hand absently across her skirt then froze, her eyes catching on the faint black smudge still clinging to her skin. The oily mark smeared when she rubbed her thumb over it, refusing to vanish. Anxiety tightened in her chest.

She slid her hand under the table, hiding it from Margaret. *Where did that come from?* Not the pews, not the casket, not anything she could remember touching. It felt foreign, wrong, like something carried home that didn't belong there.

Margaret poured her own tea and finally sat down across from her. She folded her hands around the mug, eyes on the steam rising between them. "He was proud of you, Lacy. You know that, don't you?"

The words landed heavy. Lacy nodded once, quickly, afraid her voice might break if she tried to answer. She lifted the cup to her lips, took a sip just to keep from speaking. The tea was hot, sharp with tannin, grounding her in the present while her mind spun elsewhere.

Margaret gave a small, tired smile, then reached for the sugar bowl. "It'll take time. For both of us."

Lacy held her gaze for a moment, searching for something unspoken behind it—fear, guilt, anything. But Margaret's eyes slid away, down to her mug, leaving Lacy alone with her questions and the smudge hidden under the table.

Later, after the dishes had been washed and set to dry, Lacy drifted from the kitchen. Her footsteps echoed softly on the worn floorboards, the farmhouse creaking with its own kind of memory. Margaret stayed behind, humming faintly as she shuffled through mail, giving Lacy the space she hadn't asked for but needed.

The living room smelled faintly of pipe tobacco and dust. Photographs lined the mantel and walls—sepia portraits and faded Polaroids, along with more recent frames of grandchildren at graduations and family picnics. Lacy's eyes caught on one after another. There was George kneeling beside her first bicycle, his hand steadying the seat as she wobbled down the gravel drive. Another showed him perched on a fencepost, hammer in hand while she held nails too big for her fists. Each image was a window she wanted to crawl into.

Her throat tightened as she touched the frame of one picture—an evening on the porch, George with a book open across his knees, the sun setting behind them. She could almost hear the scrape of his rocker against the boards, feel the comfort of his voice drifting through twilight. *How can a house hold so much of someone and still feel empty?*

Rain pattered against the windows, steady and unyielding, the sound blending with the creaks of settling wood. Every corner of the farmhouse seemed to sigh under the weight of absence. Lacy moved slowly, fingertips grazing furniture, her own reflection flashing faintly in the glass frames. Each memory pressed heavier against her ribs until she wasn't sure whether she wanted to cling to them or flee.

Her wandering steps brought her to the dining room. The air here felt cooler, stiller, as though the room held its breath.

The china cabinet loomed against the far wall, its glass panes reflecting the lamplight, shelves lined with George's neat stacks of plates and heirloom dishes. Lacy paused in the doorway, her pulse giving a sudden kick.

The cabinet had always been their secret. As a child, she and George had played at spies, slipping folded notes through the narrow back panel into the hidden compartment. It was their game, their code—something no one else knew. She hadn't thought about it in years, but now the memory pulsed sharp and insistent.

Her fingers itched. She glanced back toward the kitchen, hearing Margaret moving about, still shuffling papers and humming faintly. Safe. Distracted. Lacy stepped softly across the rug, knees bending as she crouched in front of the lower panel. The wood felt cool beneath her fingertips, familiar grooves guiding her hand. For a heartbeat, she froze, breath caught tight in her chest.

Don't, part of her whispered. *Leave it alone.*

But another part—stronger, restless, suspicious—pushed back. *If he left me anything, it would be here.*

With trembling fingers, she pressed along the panel's edge until she found the catch. It gave with the faintest click, the sound loud as thunder in the quiet room. Lacy's heart hammered as she eased the small door open, shadows pooling in the hidden space beyond.

Her breath hitched when her eyes found it—an envelope. Her hands shook as she reached in, the paper cool against her fingertips. She slid the envelope free and knelt there on the rug. Centered on the front of the envelope in George's firm, unmistakable handwriting were spelled two words: *For Lacy.* For a moment she couldn't move, the weight of it pressing down on her harder than the presence of the quiet house.

Finally, with trembling resolve, she opened it. The letter unfolded stiffly, its creases sharp and the ink slightly smudged where his pen had pressed too hard to the surface. At the top was a date—a little over a month ago. His voice came alive in the words, steady and grave: he insisted he had not taken his own life. He wrote of shadows in town, of men watching him, of threats he could no longer ignore. He warned her not to trust anyone—not neighbors, not officials. He said he feared for his life because of what he knew.

Lacy's pulse pounded as her eyes raced over the final lines: *If you are reading this, something is terribly wrong.*

Lacy's fingers tightened on the paper, the edges crumpling slightly. She folded it back into the envelope and slipped it deep into her pocket just as Margaret's footsteps approached from the kitchen. By the time her aunt appeared in the doorway, Lacy had risen to a crouch, one hand brushing at the rug as though to straighten it, covering her true purpose.

Margaret's eyes lingered on her. "You've been awfully quiet. Just… remembering?"

Lacy nodded, forcing a small smile. "Yeah. Just thinking about him."

Margaret stepped into the room, wiping her hands on a towel. "He kept to his routines, you know. Feeding the chickens at dawn, walking down to the creek, even when his knees gave him fits. I suppose it kept him young."

Lacy's throat ached. She wanted to ask—wanted to press. Instead, she eased into it sideways. "Did he seem… different? Toward the end?"

Margaret stilled, towel twisting between her hands. Her gaze slid toward the window, the rain streaking down the glass.

"Different how?"

"Like he was worried. Or distracted. Did he say anything?"

For a moment, Margaret's composure faltered, her lips parting as though she might confess. But then she shook her head briskly. "He was tired, Lacy. Old bones catch up, no matter how strong a man's spirit. Best not to dwell on it."

Her dismissal scraped like sandpaper. Lacy opened her mouth again, but Margaret cut her off with a sudden brightness. "I'll make us something light for dinner. You need rest after all that travel."

She turned, moving quickly back toward the kitchen. The towel hung limp from her hand, wet enough that a bead of water slid free to fall onto the floor.

Lacy stayed in the dining room, the envelope heavy against her thigh. Margaret's avoidance spoke louder than any words could. Something was being left unsaid—something George had tried to warn her about.

Later, Margaret insisted she needed to go home before it got too late. Lacy watched the taillights vanish down the gravel drive. The farmhouse fell into a deeper quiet, rain hammering against the windows. Alone at last, Lacy went upstairs to her room, the quiet pressing close around her. The air was cooler here, the hum of rain louder against the roof.

She sat on the edge of the bed, pulling the letter from her pocket with trembling hands. This time she read it slowly, absorbing every line, letting George's voice seep into her bones. Each sentence stiffened her resolve. If he had trusted her enough to leave this, she owed him the truth.

She refolded the paper with care, tucking it deep into her duffel bag beneath layers of clothes. Not the jewelry box, not the desk drawer—someplace no one would think to look. As she zipped the duffel bag shut, her reflection in the mirror caught her eye: shoulders squared, jaw tight, the soldier in her surfacing.

I'll find out what happened to you, Grandpa. I swear.

The room smelled faintly of cedar and rain, grounding her as she stood by the window. Outside, the night deepened, fields silvered by passing lightning. Thunder rolled low and steady as if echoing her vow. The farmhouse seemed to listen, holding its breath while determination settled heavy and certain in her chest.

Without warning, the house went dark in a sudden, heavy thump. The hum of the refrigerator, the tick of the clock downstairs—everything died all at once. Lacy froze, her reflection lost in the windowpane, heart lurching into her throat.

Only the storm remained. Rain lashed the glass harder, thunder rattling the panes. In the suffocating dark, she strained to hear beyond the weather, every creak of the farmhouse magnified. Was it only the storm—or something else? The silence inside pressed closer, weighted and unnatural, as though the house itself were on edge.

Lacy's pulse pounded in her ears. She stepped back from the window, the floorboard groaning under her weight. Alone, with only the storm for company, she realized the night had just shifted—from grief to danger.

Chapter 4

The wind had eased, but Lacy hadn't slept. Not really. After the power cut out, she'd sat on the edge of the bed for what felt like hours, listening to the storm drag its nails across the roof. Every groan of the old house sent her mind spiraling—floorboards creaked and wind battered the eaves, the walls settling with a tired ache. She removed the letter from her duffel bag; it felt heavier than the paper.

Gray dawn pushed through the curtains like a whisper, pale light softening the edges of the room. Rain had stopped. The silence felt almost accusatory.

She rubbed her eyes and swung her legs over the side of the bed. Her bare feet met the cool floorboards. The power was back on—the digital clock blinked *3:14* in jagged red, flashing its annoyance at the outage.

Downstairs, the refrigerator hummed again, a sound so ordinary it made her heart trip. She moved through the house carefully, checking each room. Lights clicked on. Outlets worked. No windows were broken, there was nothing obviously out of place. But the air felt wrong—like someone had been here. Or still was.

She paused at the back door, twisting the lock, testing it. Still latched. She pressed her palm flat against the back door and closed her eyes.

No signs of forced entry. No footprints on the mud-slick porch. No reason to feel this unsettled—and yet she did.

Back in the kitchen, she wrapped her fingers around the kettle's handle and filled it with water, the routine grounding her. The burner clicked on and the kettle soon began to hum with heat. Outside, the world was washed clean. Water clung to every branch, every leaf, the driveway still puddled and gleaming.

She poured hot water over a teabag and stood at the sink, watching steam rise from the mug. Her own reflection wavered in the dark windowpane—pale face, bruised eyes. The woman staring back at her looked older than she remembered.

The letter was waiting. So were the questions.

But for now, she sipped the tea slowly, letting it scald her throat just enough to remind her she was still here. Still whole. Just barely.

She brought the mug to the table and sat with George's letter beside her. The envelope lay flattened now, the flap soft from repeated openings. She slid the single page free and smoothed it with the edge of her hand.

The date at the top stared up at her—just five weeks ago. A recent past, but it felt like a message from another world.

Lacy read it again, word by word, as if it might read differently this time. The tone was careful, almost clipped, not his usual warmth. He'd written of unease, of someone watching the property. He hadn't named names, only hinted—"You know how things are in Dry Creek. Not everyone likes questions being asked." And then that line that lodged itself in her gut: *If you are' reading this, something is terribly wrong.*

She exhaled through her nose, sharp and short. This wasn't a suicide note. It was a warning.

Lacy flipped the letter over and stared at the blank back. No hidden codes, no cipher in her grandfather's looping script. But she'd learned to read between lines. He hadn't trusted anyone enough to be specific. That meant he'd feared more than just being ignored—he'd feared being silenced.

She reached for the small spiral-bound notepad she'd fished from the drawer last night. It was one of George's old backups, the kind he'd always carried in his shirt pocket and used for grocery lists, reminders, and once, a tally of every fish he and Mr. Parker had caught in a single summer. She flipped past the early pages—lists of parts, scribbled phone numbers, a doodle of a cat—and reached a blank page.

She wrote at the top in block letters: **THINGS THAT DON'T ADD UP.** Then she started working down the page.

George said he was afraid. No one mentioned that.

Letter dated five weeks ago. Why hide it?

Everyone seems too calm. Too rehearsed.

The list looked thin, but it was a start.

She tapped her pen against the paper and stared out through the window. Clouds still hung low, heavy, and slow-moving. Somewhere, the storm lingered.

She jotted one more line.

Who benefits from George being gone?

Then she closed the notebook and tucked it in her pocket, next folding the letter carefully back into the envelope. There'd be more to add. There always was.

By midmorning, she'd decided she couldn't sit with questions any longer. The will was set to be read later that afternoon, but the thought of waiting gnawed at her. George's old pickup waited in its usual spot beside the barn, streaked with rainwater and its paint dulled to the color of pewter. She climbed in, the seat cracking beneath her, and turned the key. The engine coughed, then caught—a familiar rumble that made her chest ache with memory. Better to use the hours before the lawyer's office to ask questions, to see what people weren't saying.

The drive toward town carried her past fields glazed with storm runoff and fences leaning tiredly under the weight of years. She gripped the wheel tighter with every mile. Dry Creek looked much the same, but the sight of it now brought unease instead of comfort.

She parked in front of Thomas Parker's home, a squat one-story with peeling shutters and holding a faded American flag stiff with rain. Thomas Parker, George's fishing buddy for as long as she could remember, opened the door before she reached it. He looked older, his frame more stooped, but his eyes darted nervously as if he already knew why she'd come.

"Lacy," he said, voice careful, holding the screen door half-open. "Didn't expect to see you so soon after… everything."

She nodded, steadying her breath. "I thought I should come by. Grandpa always spoke well of you."

Parker's mouth twitched, almost a smile, but it didn't reach his eyes. "He was a good man. We all miss him."

The words landed flat, rehearsed. Lacy leaned a shoulder against the porch post, studying him. "Did you notice anything different about him lately? Anything at all?"

His gaze flicked toward the yard, then back. "Can't say that I did. Old age catches up, makes a man quiet. Maybe he was just tired."

The answer slid forward too easily, like something practiced. Her gut twisted. She pressed again, gentler. "You went fishing just a few weeks ago, didn't you?"

"Mm. Sure did." His hand tightened on the doorframe. "We didn't talk much. Just sat by the water. That's how he liked it."

Silence stretched between them, filled only by the drip of water from the eaves. Lacy could almost hear the distance in his voice, as though he were reading lines handed to him.

Finally, he cleared his throat. "You take care of your aunt now. She'll need you." And with that, he pushed the screen door closed with finality.

Lacy stood on the porch a moment longer, the knot in her stomach tightening. She'd come for truth, but all she'd found was a wall of politeness—and fear she could almost taste in the air.

She drove on from Parker's place with her thoughts buzzing louder than the truck's engine. Each house she stopped at brought more of the same—neighbors and old friends answering the door with polite smiles that never touched their eyes. At one stop, Marlene Cooper pressed a slice of banana bread wrapped neatly in foil into Lacy's hands, but sidestepped every question about George's last days. Harold Atkins leaned on his porch rail, shifting from foot to foot and giving short, practiced responses before retreating inside. Others barely opened their doors at all, speaking through the cracks as though afraid to let her see too far inside.

Every word sounded cautious, rehearsed. It wasn't grief she heard—it was evasion. An undercurrent of something shared, as if the whole town had collectively agreed on a script. Lacy scribbled notes after each visit, her notebook filling with contradictions that made her gut twist tighter.

One man claimed George had been cheerful the week before his death; another said he'd been withdrawn for months. A woman swore she'd seen him at church the Sunday before;

another insisted he hadn't attended in weeks. Too many neat explanations. Too many stories that didn't line up.

By the time she pulled onto Main Street, frustration pulsed hot beneath her skin. She gripped the wheel hard enough to whiten her knuckles, her mind echoing with the same refrain: they were hiding something. And whatever it was, they were afraid to say it out loud.

Lacy slowed as she neared the corner store on Main, the truck's wipers squeaking across a windshield still dotted with mist. She swung into a space at the curb, the engine rumbling low as she shifted into park. For a moment she just sat there, eyes scanning the block. Main Street looked unchanged—same sagging awnings, same benches beneath the sycamores—but the quiet pressed in heavier than she remembered.

Movement snagged her eye. Across the street, she saw a male figure leaned against a telephone pole, hood drawn low. Even from a distance, she could feel the weight of his stare. When she reached for the door handle, his posture shifted, alert. Lacy stepped out, boots hitting the pavement, and the figure tilted his chin as if marking her every move.

She locked the truck and slung her bag over her shoulder. By the time she looked back, the figure had pushed away from the pole. He slipped behind the corner of the store, disappearing into the narrow alley without a sound. The space he'd left seemed suddenly colder.

A prickle ran up her spine. Someone was watching her—and they didn't want to be seen.

The diner's neon sign flickered halfheartedly as Lacy stepped through its door. It had been one of George's favorite places, a spot where he'd met friends for coffee and pie after Sunday service. The bell above the door jingled, drawing every pair of eyes in the place toward her entrance for a heartbeat before they slid away again. The air smelled of fried food and coffee that had been left on the burner too long. Vinyl booths lined the walls, most empty, and a few locals hunched over their plates, murmuring low.

A waitress with graying hair pulled back tight introduced herself as Sandy. "Sit anywhere you like," she said, voice polite but brisk. Lacy slid onto a stool at the counter. Sandy poured her coffee without being asked, the mug chipped at the rim.

"Thanks," Lacy murmured, wrapping her hands around the warmth. She could feel the hush ripple behind her, conversation thinning until it was little more than a hum. The weight of their stares pressed against her back.

Sandy busied herself at the register, not asking questions. Not making small talk. The kind of silence that said more than words could.

Lacy sipped, bitter coffee burning her tongue, and tried to focus on the ordinary—the hiss of the griddle, the scrape of forks against plates. But the undercurrent was undeniable. This was no welcome home. It was a warning in the shape of avoidance.

When she finished, she slid cash under the edge of the mug and rose. Stepping outside, she let the door swing shut behind her. The street was quiet again, the only movement the sway of the diner's sign in the damp breeze.

Upon making it back to the truck, she spotted something that stopped her cold. Tucked under the windshield wiper was a scrap of paper, folded once. She glanced up and down the street; no one lingered, but the hairs on her neck lifted all the same. With careful fingers, she plucked the note free and unfolded it.

The message was scrawled in jagged ink: **Leave it alone, or**

you'll end up like him.

Her breath caught, the words vibrating through her chest. The paper shook in her grip as she read them again. Whoever had left this hadn't just wanted to frighten her—they'd wanted to make sure she knew exactly what line she was crossing.

The paper felt like ice in her hand. Lacy folded it slowly, slipping it into her jacket pocket as if hiding it might dull its sting. She leaned against the truck door, letting the drizzle bead across her hairline, eyes sweeping the street for any hint of movement. Nothing but still storefronts and the sway of the diner's sign. Whoever had left the note was long gone.

She climbed into the cab, heart hammering harder than when she'd faced Parker's hollow eyes. The warning's sharp edges pushed at her ribs.

She drove to the lawyer's office, rain-slick streets flashing past. Margaret's pickup was already in the lot when she arrived. Inside, the office was lined with oak shelves and thick carpet that muffled every footstep. The receptionist led Lacy to the attorney's office, where Margaret sat stiffly in a wingback chair across from the attorney's desk, her hands folded tight in her lap. She looked up when Lacy entered, relief mingled with unease in her eyes.

The lawyer, Mr. Denton, adjusted his glasses and cleared his throat. "Thank you both for coming. This shouldn't take long." He opened a folder thick with papers. "Mr. Peterson's affairs were in order. The farmhouse and land have been left to you, Miss Krammer."

Lacy's stomach tightened, her gaze flicking toward Margaret, bracing for resentment. But her aunt only gave a weary nod. "George wanted you to have it. He knew what it meant to you."

Mr. Denton continued, detailing accounts and assets that

had gone to Margaret. Lacy tried to follow, but her mind kept circling back to the note in her pocket, the unseen eyes in the street.

When the meeting wrapped, Margaret rose quickly, gathering her purse. "We'll talk later," she murmured, brushing Lacy's arm before stepping out into the hall.

Lacy started to follow, but Mr. Denton stopped her with a small gesture. From beneath his desk, he produced and slid a large manila envelope across the polished wood surface. "This was left with instructions for you, privately. George wanted you to have it, though he gave no explanation."

The envelope was heavier than she expected, sealed tight. She slipped it into her bag, her pulse quickening. Another secret, waiting to be opened.

Lacy stepped back out into the gray afternoon, the manila envelope secure in her bag. The town hall clock across the square tolled the hour, its chime carrying over the quiet streets. She paused on the steps, drawing in a breath to steady herself. But the moment she turned toward the parking lot, she caught sight of a familiar figure waiting by the corner: Marcus Bell, the journalist from the church.

He tipped his head in greeting, rain beading off the edge of his umbrella. "Sergeant Krammer," he said, his tone polite but edged with curiosity. "Mind if I walk with you a moment?"

Her shoulders stiffened. "I'm not giving interviews."

"I figured you'd say that." He fell into step beside her anyway, his voice low enough not to carry. "But you should know—your grandfather wasn't just loved. He was respected, and respect like that makes enemies. I've been following stories like this for months."

Lacy kept her gaze ahead, unlocking the truck. "I don't know what you're talking about."

Marcus offered a thin smile, pulling a battered notebook out from his coat. He flipped it open, its pages soft from use. "I know I already gave you one of these at the church," he said, sliding another business card free, "but in case that one's gone missing, here's another. When you're ready to talk, I'll be around."

She accepted the card with a curt nod, tucking it deep into her pocket. His persistence needled her, but beneath it she caught something else—concern. Whether it was genuine or calculated, she couldn't tell. Not yet.

"Drive safe," he said, stepping back as she climbed into the cab. His eyes lingered on her bag, on the envelope hidden within, before he turned and walked away, scribbling something into his notebook.

The truck's engine rumbled to life. Lacy gripped the wheel tighter than necessary. Secrets and warnings were piling up faster than she could sort through them—and now a stranger wanted in on them too.

The drive back toward the farmhouse was slow, the wipers pushing aside a mist that clung stubbornly to the windshield. Lacy kept one eye on the rearview mirror, pulse quickening each time a vehicle appeared behind her. For several miles, a dark sedan hovered two car-lengths back from her, refusing to pass. Her grip on the wheel tightened until the leather creaked. She shifted lanes, slowed at a turn—and still it followed.

Finally, just outside Dry Creek's edge, the sedan blinked its signal and turned down a side road, vanishing into the trees. Relief should have come after that, but it didn't. The hollowness in her chest stayed put.

When she pulled into the drive, the farmhouse loomed quiet, its white paint dampened to gray in the drizzle. She cut the engine and sat listening to the tick of cooling metal. Something felt off. Lacy could see that the porch light she'd left off was now glowing faintly against the rain. Her stomach dropped.

She climbed out with her bag slung over her shoulder, boots crunching gravel, and scanned the yard. Nothing moved. Still, the air seemed charged, much like it had when the power had gone out. She mounted the steps slowly, each board groaning under her weight. At the top, her breath stalled. The front door stood ajar, a thin crack of shadow between frame and latch. She was sure she'd locked it behind her that morning.

Lacy pushed the door forward with her fingertips. It creaked wider into darkness. Her heart hammered in her ears as she stood frozen on the threshold, every instinct screaming that whatever waited inside had changed the house she thought she knew.

Chapter 5

Lacy froze at the entrance, one hand braced against the doorframe. The sight jolted her pulse, every muscle coiled tight. For a moment, she simply stood there, caught between stepping forward and retreating, the weight of the unknown pressing down on her chest. At last, she stepped into the darkened hall, setting her bag down by the front door before moving farther in, boots silent on the worn runner. The smell of last night's storm clung to the air. Every corner felt too still, too expectant.

She moved room by room, flicking on lights as she went. The living room—unchanged, the afghan folded just as she remembered. The kitchen—tidy, the kettle gleaming on the stove. Her grandfather's boots, toes scuffed, remained by the door exactly where they'd always been. Nothing seemed out of place, but her nerves buzzed, unwilling to believe it.

She crept up the stairs, each tread creaking under her weight. The hall stretched narrow and dim, lined with framed photos that watched her pass. She paused at her bedroom door, pressing her palm against the door before nudging it open. The quilt on the bed lay undisturbed. Her duffel bag sat slouched where she'd left it. Still, the prickle at the base of her neck refused to ease.

After another sweep of the rooms, she returned to the foyer, drawing in a shaky breath. With deliberate care, she closed the front door and locked it, testing it twice to be sure. The metallic click echoed too loudly in the quiet house.

She leaned back against the door, heart thundering. Maybe no one had been inside. Maybe the storm had rattled the old latch loose. But the memory of the vehicles in her rearview mirror lingered, souring the air in her lungs.

The farmhouse had always been her safe place. Now it felt like a trap with shadows at every corner.

She pushed away from the door, scooped up her bag, and crossed to the kitchen. The envelope's weight already tugged at her thoughts as she set her bag on a chair and unzipped it with fingers that wouldn't quite steady.

The sealed manila envelope waited inside, its flap unbroken. She had carried it like a stone since the lawyer had handed it over, resisting the urge to tear into it on the spot. Now, alone in the house, she couldn't put it off any longer.

She pulled the manila envelope from her bag, set it down, and laid it flat on the scarred wood. For a long moment she only stared at it, palms pressed to the surface on either side. What if it held nothing useful? What if it was worse than she imagined? The urge to leave it sealed battled against the compulsion to know. Then her grandfather's voice rose in memory—steady, uncompromising: *Always face the truth, no matter how hard it hits.*

With a sharp breath, she slid her thumb under the flap. The paper gave with a reluctant tear. Inside lay a stack of documents thick enough to bow the envelope: official reports, brittle pages stamped with county seals, letters typed on yellowing bond. Intermixed were photographs—black-and-white portraits of people she half-recognized from town and others unfamiliar, their eyes caught mid-blink or narrowed against the sun. Some documents bore handwritten notes across the margins.

On top of the pile rested a single sheet, folded once, with names typed in columns. Her eyes skimmed down the list: Parker, Yates, Crawford, Wilkes… others she didn't know. She whispered each under her breath, tasting the weight of them, the names of families that had stood in Dry Creek for generations. Why had her grandfather kept this? Why give it to her?

Her pulse throbbed as she sorted through the rest—official documents marked "confidential," fragments of legal correspondence, records of land transfers, death certificates. Threads of stories dangled from every page, waiting to be tied together. She pressed her palm over the stack as if to hold it in place, fighting the dread that each sheet carried pieces of something too large for her to understand yet.

Whatever secrets George had carried to his grave, they were here now, staring up at her from the table and demanding she take them on.

A sudden rap on the front door shattered the stillness. The sound ricocheted through the quiet house, sharp as a gunshot. Lacy flinched, papers sliding under her hand. Her throat went dry. She hadn't heard a car pull up.

She rose slowly, every nerve on edge, and moved to the front window. Peering through the curtain, she caught sight of a tall figure on the porch, dark coat beaded with rain. In one hand he held an umbrella, in the other a folded newspaper. Her breath eased fractionally when recognition struck—Marcus Bell.

Another knock, lighter this time. "Ms. Krammer?" His voice carried through the wood, polite but steady. "Sorry to come by unannounced."

Lacy hesitated at the door, hand hovering over the knob.

How much had he seen? Her instinct screamed for caution. At last, she pulled the door open a few inches, chain still latched. "What do you want?"

Marcus held the umbrella closed by his side, his eyes narrowing against the drizzle. "Just to check on you. And… maybe to talk." He lifted the folded newspaper slightly, as though it were proof of something. "Could I come in for a moment?"

Her pulse hammered, torn between slamming the door and hearing him out. George's letter echoed in her mind—*Don't trust anyone.* And yet Marcus's gaze held something that wasn't idle curiosity. It was sharper, more insistent, as if he carried questions too heavy to leave unasked.

Lacy unlatched the chain and opened the door fully, but kept her stance guarded. "You've picked a strange time to pay a visit."

He offered a rueful smile. "There's no good time for this kind of thing. May I?"

For a heartbeat, neither of them moved. Then Lacy stepped aside just enough to let him cross the threshold, the unease in her chest only deepening as the rain pattered harder against the porch roof.

Marcus glanced around the entryway as he stepped inside, taking in the stack of papers still scattered across the kitchen table. "I didn't mean to intrude," he said, lowering his voice as though wary of the walls themselves. "But I figured it was better to come straight to you than keep circling around town chasing whispers."

Lacy closed the door firmly behind him, folding her arms. "Whispers about what?" Her tone carried more bite than she'd intended it to, sharpened by fatigue and the raw edge of fear.

He lifted a shoulder, almost casual, though the tightness in his jaw betrayed the effort. "About your grandfather. About the way people are already rewriting his story." He tapped the newspaper in his hand. "Obituaries are supposed to be tributes. But this one reads more like a closing argument—suicide, end of case. No mention of who he really was, or what he meant to this place."

Her chest tightened. She thought of George's letter, the urgency in his final words. "Maybe that's the version people want to believe."

Marcus studied her, his gaze uncomfortably steady. "And you? Is that the version you believe?"

Lacy looked away, the silence between them stretching thin. The documents on the table seemed to hum with their own presence, daring her to speak. At last, she shook her head once, almost imperceptibly. "No," she admitted. "I don't."

His eyes slightly softened. He shifted the folded newspaper in his hand, his gaze flicking toward the kitchen, though he didn't move closer. "Then maybe we're on the same side."

Lacy narrowed her eyes, measuring his words. The phrase landed too easily, like something rehearsed. She stepped past him into the kitchen, gathering the papers into a neater pile, needing the barrier of motion to steady herself. Marcus followed at a distance, stopping short of the table as if wary of intruding on sacred ground.

"So that's it?" she asked, fingers aligning the edges of the documents. "You show up on my porch, say we're on the same side, and I'm supposed to believe you?"

Marcus stood steadily, his coat dripping faintly onto the floorboards. "Not supposed to. Just hoping you might." He hesitated, then added, "I've been keeping tabs since the news broke. Your grandfather's death didn't sit right with me. Too neat. Too convenient."

Her breath caught, a bitter satisfaction mixing with unease. "You think it wasn't suicide."

"I think Dry Creek has more shadows than folks care to admit," Marcus replied, his tone even but edged. "And if George Peterson stirred some of them up, well, people might prefer to bury the truth with him."

Lacy's hand hovered over the stack, resisting the urge to reveal the names, the documents, the letter once again hidden away in her duffel upstairs. "And what is it you want from me?"

He met her gaze squarely. "The same thing you want: answers. But you don't trust me yet—and that's fair. Still, you're not going to find them alone."

His words pricked at the raw place inside her that had been growing since the funeral—the hollow certainty that something was wrong and the town had closed ranks. She hated the truth of it, hated that she needed anyone at all. But the idea of someone else carrying part of the weight was tempting, dangerous as it felt.

She exhaled slowly, the farmhouse creaking in the pause. "Then we'll see if our sides really line up."

Marcus stepped closer at last, his eyes flicking to the papers before returning to her face. "Why don't we take a look together? Maybe something here will make sense to me that doesn't to you. Or the other way around."

Lacy studied him for a beat longer, then pulled out a chair. "Sit. But this doesn't mean I trust you. It means I want to see what you know."

He nodded once and eased into the seat, laying his notebook beside the pile. Its cover was scuffed, corners bent from long use. Lacy recognized the kind of dedication it took to keep notes like that—habit born from years of watching and recording.

She pushed the top page toward him, the list of names. "Recognize any?"

Marcus scanned it, lips tightening as he traced the columns with his finger. "A few. Crawford—there was a fire on their property fifteen years back. No one ever proved arson, but I've always wondered. Wilkes—daughter went missing. Official line was she ran off, but I interviewed a classmate who swore otherwise." He tapped one more. "Yates. That name's come up in more than one story I chased, always on the edges."

The room seemed to shrink as his words piled weight on the names. Lacy pulled another sheet free, one of the death certificates, sliding it across the wood. "George kept all of this for a reason. He wanted me to see it."

Marcus met her gaze again. "Then he was passing you the torch."

The thought made her chest constrict. She had wanted answers, not a burden. Yet here it was laid out on the scarred table between them, too heavy to push aside.

They worked through the stack slowly, the kitchen clock ticking louder with every turn of a page. Marcus scribbled quick notes in his battered notebook, pausing often to cross-reference things. The further they went, the clearer the pattern became: sudden deaths, unexplained disappearances, and tragedies written off as accidents, each one connected by a thread too fine for the official record but undeniable in the details George had saved.

Lacy leaned forward, pointing to a clipping about a warehouse fire. "This was right before the Crawfords' barn burned. Same month, different side of the county. Both called 'accidents.'"

Marcus's brow furrowed as he flipped to another page in his notebook. "And both insured by the same company. One that happens to have ties to the sheriff's office." He tapped his pen against the margin. "It's not proof, but it's a pattern. Someone wanted these cases buried."

The air in the kitchen seemed to thicken. Lacy felt the weight of her grandfather's intent in every page—he'd left her a trail, trusting she'd follow. Her stomach knotted at the thought. She wasn't trained for this, not really. But she was already in too deep to walk away now.

She shoved a hand through her hair, frustration biting at her. "This is bigger than I thought. And more dangerous."

Marcus looked up, his expression grim but resolute. "That's why we don't go at it alone. George must've known someone would try to silence him. He left this for you because he trusted you could finish what he started."

The words settled heavy in her chest. For the first time since she'd stepped foot back in Dry Creek, Lacy felt the fragile outline of something beginning to form: partnership, yes, but also a fight neither of them could afford to lose.

The phone on the wall rang, its sharp peal startling in the silence. Lacy flinched, her hand tightening on the edge of the table. Marcus glanced at her, eyebrows raised. "You going to get that?"

She rose slowly, every instinct on alert, and crossed to the phone. The receiver felt cold in her hand as she lifted it. "Hello?"

"Lacy?" Margaret's voice, tight and worried. Relief warred with fresh unease. "I just wanted to check on you. I heard folks talking in town... saying you've been asking questions. Be careful. Some people don't take kindly to digging."

Lacy pressed her lips together, fighting the urge to look back at Marcus. "I'm fine, Aunt Margaret. Just sorting through some of Grandpa's things."

There was a pause, then Margaret's voice dropped lower, as if she didn't want anyone to overhear. "Promise me you'll be careful. I don't want you caught up in anything dangerous."

"I promise," Lacy said, though the words felt hollow. She replaced the receiver, her chest tight. When she turned, Marcus was watching her, his expression unreadable.

"Family worried?" he asked softly.

"Something like that," she murmured, forcing herself to sit again. The echo of Margaret's warning lingered, heavier than the stack of papers between them.

Lacy tried to focus back on the documents, but Margaret's words echoed like a warning bell. The farmhouse suddenly seemed too quiet, the shadows in the corners pressing closer. Marcus closed his notebook with a quiet snap and tucked it under his arm.

"You've got enough to chew on for tonight," he said, rising. "Lock your doors. I'll be in touch."

She followed him to the door, watching as he stepped out into the night. The sound of his footsteps faded down the gravel drive until only the hum of crickets remained. Lacy shut the door, turning the lock with deliberate care, then gathered the documents from the kitchen table and placed them back in the envelope. With trembling hands, she walked to the dining room and slipped the envelope into the china cabinet's secret compartment, easing the panel shut.

Later, upstairs in her room, she tried to rest. Darkness pressed close, the house settling around her in uneasy silence. Just as her eyelids began to drift, light swept suddenly across the wall. Headlights. They lingered, flooding her window in harsh white, idling in place before slowly pulling away. Lacy lay rigid, pulse hammering, certain now that someone was watching, waiting, and that the farmhouse was no longer hers alone.

Chapter 6

Lacy hadn't truly slept, not in the way that restored anything. She'd spent most of the night half-sitting against the headboard, her ears tuned to every creak, every gust of wind brushing the windows. The memory of headlights sweeping across her room still pulsed behind her eyes. Once, she could've sworn she'd seen a shape—a shoulder, maybe—just beyond the glass. But when she snapped the curtain aside, there was nothing outside but the dark and the quiet hum of rain.

Dawn seeped in pale and slow, turning the ceiling faintly gold. She pushed the covers back and stood, joints stiff with fatigue. From her window, the yard looked undisturbed. No tire tracks in the gravel. No muddy footprints. Still, unease clung to her like a film she couldn't wash off.

Downstairs, the house felt cooler, as if it too had held its breath overnight. She made a slow circuit through the rooms, checking locks and curtains, peering out each window. The front door remained bolted. Also the back door. Nothing was broken, nothing shifted from the way she'd left it. Even so, she double-checked the latch on the back windows and pressed her palm to the cool glass, listening.

Silence.

But it wasn't peace.

In the kitchen, she let the kettle hum while she leaned on the counter, palms braced, watching the steam rise. Her reflection stared back at her in the dark window over the sink, hollow-eyed and tight-lipped.

This was the cost of digging. Of asking. Of staying.

She poured her tea and wrapped both hands around the mug, letting the heat soak into her fingers. There were no answers this morning, but the questions hadn't gone anywhere.

And neither, apparently, had whoever had been watching.

She carried the mug with her into the dining room, the silence ticking beside her like a clock she couldn't hear. At the china cabinet, she crouched and slid open the lower panel again, fingers feeling for the narrow lip of the hidden compartment. Her grandfather had built it himself, tucked behind the false back of the lowest shelf. *A spot for emergency cash,* he used to say. But what he'd left her was heavier.

The manila envelope was still there, cool to the touch.

Lacy eased it out and brought it to the kitchen table, setting it down with her tea. She didn't sit right away. She stood with her hands braced on the back of the chair, staring at the envelope as if it might open on its own.

She sat and pulled it open.

The papers inside had shifted from her last review with Marcus. She spread them out again—photocopies of reports with blurred stamps, handwritten memos in cramped cursive, court filings, property deeds, old letters. She laid them out in clusters across the table, trying to find a shape in the chaos.

A folded page near the bottom caught her eye: legal stationery, clipped from something larger. At first glance, it seemed like more of the same—a list of contacts, maybe, or a chain of signatures. But in the top corner, in neat block print, was something she hadn't noticed before:

P.O. Box 1127 – R.P.H.

She stared at the initials. They didn't mean anything. Not yet. But her stomach twisted anyway.

She flipped her notepad open and jotted it down: **R.P.H.** Could be a name, a business, anything. She underlined it twice, then started a fresh list: things she and Marcus hadn't discussed. Threads that were left dangling. One page became two.

Her tea had gone cold, but she didn't notice. The farmhouse groaned softly in the quiet, the wind brushing the eaves like someone thinking about knocking.

Whatever George had uncovered, he hadn't gone quietly. And now it was her turn to decide how much noise she was willing to make.

Lacy stepped out onto the porch, mug in hand, steam rising faintly from the fresh brew. The morning air carried the scent of damp earth and woodsmoke from somewhere down the road. It should have been calming. Should have felt like a fresh start. But her shoulders were still drawn tight and her eyes kept drifting to the edges of the trees.

She sipped once, then headed down the steps, gravel crunching beneath her boots as she crossed to the mailbox. It stood just beyond the fence line, leaning slightly from years of frost heave. She flipped the lid open more out of routine than expectation—no one in town had reason to write her.

A single envelope sat inside, stark white against the black metal.

No stamp. No address.

A chill pricked up the back of her neck.

She pulled it free. The paper felt stiff, heavier than standard stock. Her name wasn't on it, but somehow she knew it was meant for her. She peeled the flap back with slow fingers, each tear of the glue sounding louder than it should.

Inside was a single sheet of paper.

The message was short, assembled from magazine clippings, each letter snipped and glued with uneven care:

YOU AREN'T WANTED HERE. GO AWAY.

The mug slipped from her hand and struck the gravel with a dull crack, porcelain splintering in a fan across the ground. Tea soaked into the stones.

Lacy didn't move. Her heart banged hard against her ribs, breath shallow in her throat. The note shook in her grip, but she read it again—just to be sure.

Not imagined.

Not subtle.

She scanned the road, the trees, the fields beyond. No cars. No watchers. Just the wind nudging branches like fingers tapping on a doorframe.

But someone had been close enough to deliver this. Close enough to know her routines.

She folded the note with deliberate care and tucked it into her jacket pocket, the glue rough against her fingertips. Then she gathered up the broken mug pieces and carried them back to the house, dropping them into the metal trash bin with a hollow clang.

Only once she was back inside with the door locked behind her did she lean against it, breath caught in her chest.

This wasn't just a warning.

It was a promise.

Just as Lacy was making a fresh cup of tea, she heard a sharp knock coming from the front door.

She jumped, breath catching in her throat. She wiped her hands on a dish towel and moved cautiously to the window, angling the curtain just enough to see.

Margaret stood on the porch, arms wrapped tightly around herself, her expression tight with worry.

Lacy let out a breath and opened the door. "Hey. Everything okay?"

Margaret's eyes scanned her face. "I was about to ask you the same."

Lacy stepped aside. "Come in."

Margaret entered, her gaze drifting over the kitchen, the hallway, the corners. "You've got everyone talking."

Lacy arched a brow. "That didn't take long."

"Small town," Margaret said simply. "People notice. And they talk."

Lacy poured a fresh cup of tea and handed it to her aunt. "I'm fine. Just... sorting things out."

Margaret took the mug but didn't drink. "There's more than just rumors going around, Lace. Someone said you've been asking about George."

Lacy studied her. "I have."

Margaret hesitated. "Then I'll ask you directly. Are you in trouble?"

Lacy opened her mouth. Closed it. Looked away. "I don't know. Not yet."

Margaret reached out and touched her hand. "Be careful. Please. Some things in this town don't stay buried just because we pretend not to see them."

Lacy met her eyes. "That's exactly why I can't stop looking."

After Margaret left, Lacy stood by the kitchen window, hands wrapped around the cooling mug of tea. The silence pressed in again, heavy and close. Her aunt's parting words echoed louder now—*Be careful. Some things don't stay buried.*

That's when the memory cracked through. Not a full scene at first—just flashes.

She was twenty again, in her junior year of college.

The office was small. Quiet. Just her and the professor, whose praise had always come with a hand on her shoulder. A glance that lingered. An invitation to office hours she didn't want to accept.

He closed the door behind her. Locked it.

His voice stayed calm. Measured. So did hers—at first.

Then his hand was on her wrist. His breath on her cheek. Her back hitting the wall.

She'd shoved him. Hard.

She remembered the scrape of his belt against her hand. The sour smell of his cologne. The press of his body, and her own heart trying to hammer its way out of her ribs.

And then—just as suddenly—she'd been outside again. Backpack half-zipped. Steps too fast across the quad.

She'd reported it.

Nothing had happened.

They said she'd misunderstood. That she'd led him on. That it would ruin *his* career.

That she should let it go.

So she did. She let it all go.

She left school two weeks later. Joined the Army. Reinvented herself one mile at a time.

And she hadn't cried since.

Not really. Not like that.

Even now, there were no tears. Just the burn in her throat. The hot ache in her chest. The memory of silence and the promise of never being silenced again.

Because this town felt the same.

Different faces. Same rules.

And she wasn't that girl anymore.

Not now.

A sudden sound broke the silence.

Lacy went still, her mug paused midair.

There it was again—a faint creak, then a dull thunk. Not inside. At the back of the house.

She moved quietly through the kitchen, setting the mug in the sink without a sound. Her heartbeat thudded in her ears as she crept to the mudroom and unlocked the back door. She didn't open it right away. Instead, she pressed her ear to the wood and held her breath.

Another sound. A faint scrape. Then nothing.

She eased the door open an inch. The yard beyond looked the same—wind teasing the overgrown grass, sun slanting through the trees. But something was wrong.

The stoop.

A footprint. Muddy. Fresh.

She stepped outside, gaze sweeping the yard, the fence line, the tree line. No movement. No figures darting through the brush. But the air buzzed with the feeling of having just missed someone.

Her eyes dropped back to the stoop.

Another mark. Right at the edge of the doorframe. She leaned over, fingers brushing the shallow groove in the wood.

Pry marks.

Lacy straightened slowly, the breath leaving her lungs in a hard exhale.

Someone had tried to get in. While she was home. Maybe

while she was sitting in the kitchen, tea cooling in her hands. Maybe while she was staring at nothing, lost in memory.

The thought sent a tremor through her, but it didn't buckle her.

She turned and walked the perimeter, boots silent in the grass, checking every window, every entrance. The tracks disappeared around the side of the house, fading into gravel where the ground dried out. But the intent had been clear.

This wasn't a warning.

This was a test.

She stood at the back steps again, staring down at the prints. Something hard settled in her chest, cold and immovable.

They wanted her afraid. Shaken.

They weren't going to get that.

Not anymore.

She stepped back inside, locked the door, and slid the deadbolt.

She had locks to replace.

And she wasn't waiting.

Lacy parked close to the hardware store's side entrance and shut off the engine, the truck ticking in the silence that followed. A small display window showcased some rusted tools—and beside them, a faded flyer for last year's harvest fair, its edges curled from sun and time. She sat a moment longer, hand resting on the key, steeling herself.

Inside, the store was cooler than she expected. The scent of motor oil and cedar hung in the air. A bell above the door jingled behind her, sharp in the stillness.

Three men stood near the counter, their heads bent in conversation. One wore overalls and work boots, another a Carhartt jacket. As soon as she stepped in, the conversation halted. The silence spread thick as syrup.

They didn't stare, not exactly. But they didn't greet her either. One man muttered something and turned toward the paint aisle. Another busied himself with the display of garden gloves.

Lacy kept her spine straight and her gaze forward as she moved past them. The deadbolts were in Aisle 3, the same place they'd always been. She pulled two from the rack, then grabbed a pack of screws and a pry bar—just in case.

At the register, the clerk barely looked up. Gary Dodd, wiry and grizzled, had rung up her grandfather's purchases for decades. Today, he scanned the items with mechanical motions, not meeting her eyes.

"How's your mother doin'?" he asked, tone neutral.

"She passed two years ago," Lacy said evenly.

Gary's lips twitched. "Right. Sorry. Been a while."

He didn't ask about George. Didn't ask how the house was or if she needed help with the installation. Just told her the total, bagged the items, and slid the receipt across the counter without another word.

Outside again, Lacy paused at the edge of the sidewalk. Her gaze swept the storefronts—most windows empty or dark. She'd grown up in this town. Walked these streets as a child. But now the familiar was turning foreign, faces unreadable and greetings withheld.

They knew something. Or they feared it.

She loaded the supplies into the truck and climbed behind the wheel. The weight in her chest had shifted. No longer fear.

Resolve. Cold and sharp.

They didn't want her here?

Good.

That meant she was getting close.

By the time she pulled up the gravel drive, the sun was low and the farmhouse windows glinted like watching eyes. She unloaded the supplies and went room to room, checking every latch, every frame.

Her cell phone rang just as she was locking the last window.

She jumped, heart kicking up a notch as she crossed the room and picked it up from the counter, glancing at the screen.

Marcus.

She answered with a clipped "Yeah?"

"I've got something," he said. His voice was low, urgent—not the easy tone he used to coax people open. "A name."

Lacy leaned against the kitchen counter. "I'm listening."

"You remember that list of former deputies tucked in with the land files? I dug into one name that didn't have a forwarding address: Craig Tolbert. Left the sheriff's office about four years ago. No resignation letter, no pension draw. Just gone."

Lacy frowned. "That's odd."

"More than that," Marcus said. "He left right after a complaint was filed—something internal, no details. And get this—he co-signed a property loan with George five months before he vanished."

Her stomach dropped. "You're sure?"

"Positive. It's buried deep, but the signature's there."

"Where is he now?"

"Don't know, it's like he just vanished. I'll keep digging."

Lacy pinched the bridge of her nose. "So George was working with someone inside the sheriff's department… and that someone disappeared under pressure."

"Looks that way."

She exhaled slowly. "It's unraveling, Marcus. I can feel it. First the threats. Now this? Someone's trying to shut this down—

hard."

There was a pause on the line, then Marcus's voice returned softer. "You need to be careful, Lacy. This isn't just a land squabble or some old scandal. It's deeper. Rot that goes back years."

"I know." She looked out the window toward the tree line, now blurred in the fading light. "But I'm not backing down."

"We'll figure this out," Marcus said. "I'll keep working the Tolbert angle. We'll meet in the morning?"

"Yeah."

"Lock up tight tonight."

She hung up and set the phone down, her reflection catching faintly in the dark glass of the window—blurred, but steady.

Tomorrow, they'd dig deeper.

Tonight, she'd hold the line.

She triple-checked each lock before drawing the curtains tight. The new deadbolts clicked into place with a satisfying finality, but it didn't chase off the knot in her gut. Not entirely.

The night had deepened, quiet settling over the house in thick folds. Still, she couldn't shake the urge to see it all for herself.

Grabbing her flashlight from the drawer, she slipped out the back door, careful to close it softly behind her. The beam cut a narrow path through the dark, catching the glint of dew on grass and the warped edge of the rusted rain barrel. In the distance, a lone owl called out, the sound too high and clean in the hush.

She moved along the side of the house, gravel crunching beneath her boots, scanning each window and corner. Everything looked the same. But her skin crawled anyway.

At the far edge of the porch, something caught her eye.

She moved closer, angling the flashlight down.

Footprints. Fresh ones.

The same size and shape as the ones she'd found that morning—narrow, deep heel. They trailed past the back stoop, then veered along the side of the house.

Lacy followed them to the edge of the gravel, where the prints vanished.

She swung the light in a slow arc across the field beyond.

Nothing.

Still, the sense of being watched pressed in around her, tighter now.

She turned back, sweeping the flashlight one last time across the yard, holding her breath.

Nothing moved.

But the footprints were real.

This wasn't fear anymore.

It was fuel.

Chapter 7

The morning sun filtered through a thin veil of clouds as Lacy stepped out onto the farmhouse porch, keys in one hand and bag over her shoulder. The air still held a chill, and the gravel drive sparkled with dew. She paused for a moment, scanning the yard—no new footprints, no signs of movement—before descending the steps and climbing into the pickup.

The engine turned over with a familiar groan, and she let it idle while she adjusted the mirrors. Her nerves hadn't eased much overnight despite the new locks and double-checked windows. Still, routine was something. And today, routine meant meeting Marcus.

The drive was uneventful, the two-lane road flanked by brittle cornstalks and the occasional mailbox leaning like a tired sentinel.

She turned off the main road just past the faded billboard advertising last year's livestock festival and pulled into the gravel lot beside the café. Only one other vehicle sat in the lot: a dark sedan with its hood still ticking with heat.

The café sat just outside the edge of town, its windows dimmed by sun-bleached blinds and a neon "Open" sign that blinked like it wasn't sure it meant it. Lacy parked beside the sedan and took a breath before stepping out of the pickup and into the diner's hushed clatter. The place smelled of coffee and bacon, a waitress with tired eyes offering her a nod as she slid into the booth Marcus was already seated at.

Marcus had a mug of coffee in front of him, steam curling faintly toward the ceiling fan overhead. His notebook lay open beside it, pages scrawled with tight, looping script.

"You look like you didn't sleep," he said.

Lacy offered a tight smile. "Did you?"

He didn't answer. She didn't expect him to.

She wrapped her hands around a mug the waitress set in front of her. "Someone was outside the house last night. Footprints—fresh ones. Same kind as before."

Marcus's expression didn't change, but his fingers tightened around his pen.

"You report it?"

She shook her head. "Didn't see the point. Whoever it was is long gone, and I don't trust the sheriff's office to take it seriously."

"Fair," Marcus said. He flipped a page in his notebook. "I did some digging on former deputy Craig Tolbert. Resigned suddenly about four years ago. No formal statement. The timing lines up too neatly with when George stopped logging new research in his files."

Lacy frowned. "You think they knew each other?"

"If they didn't, I'd be shocked. Tolbert was assigned to a lot of the same cases George kept copies of. Including that string of missing persons cases from the early 2000s."

The waitress returned with their plates: eggs, toast, and something attempting to be hash browns. They both waited until she moved on before Marcus continued.

"There's something else," he said, lowering his voice. "I found an archived article from the *Dry Creek Ledger*—editorial, buried deep. A local business owner claimed there was a cover-up involving missing files and hush money."

"What happened to him?"

"He retracted the statement a week later. Said it was a misunderstanding. And then sold the business six months after."

Lacy pushed her eggs around her plate, appetite gone. "So we have a deputy who vanished, a bunch of cases no one talks about, and locals getting scared off."

"And someone watching your house."

The diner's buzz dimmed to a hush for a moment before conversation picked back up. Lacy leaned forward.

"We need to map this. Everything we have—connections, names, dates. Lay it all out. There has to be a pattern."

Marcus nodded slowly. "What we need are the police reports Tolbert was working on."

"That means going to the sheriff's office," Lacy added. "Do you think they would give them to us?"

"Only one way to find out," Marcus answered.

Outside, a delivery truck rumbled past the window, trailing dust. Inside, the tension between them had shifted—not fear, not yet resolve, but something more dangerous: conviction.

They left the café not long after and headed toward the county seat, Madisonville, a thirty-minute drive away. Lacy followed Marcus's sedan, her truck trailing at a cautious distance.

The sheriff's office stood half a block from the County Courthouse, squat and square, with peeling trim and a lopsided American flag out front. Lacy parked beside a blue patrol SUV and waited for Marcus to join her before stepping inside.

The office air smelled faintly of mildew and old coffee. A

uniformed deputy—young, blond, and visibly bored—glanced up from her computer screen.

"We're here to ask about some old case files," Marcus said to him, polite but firm. "Missing persons from the early 2000s. Files that Deputy Craig Tolbert may have worked on."

The deputy's face shuttered. "You'll need to speak with the sheriff."

"Is he available?"

She didn't answer, just buzzed the back and returned to scrolling.

After a few minutes, Sheriff Harold "Hal" Boyette emerged from the hallway. Broader than Lacy remembered from her childhood visits, his badge tilted on his chest like an afterthought.

"Well, now," he said, flashing a grin. "If it isn't George Peterson's granddaughter. I thought I heard you were back."

Lacy straightened. "We're looking into cases Deputy Tolbert may have handled before he left town. We've come across references in town documents that mention his name—enough to raise questions."

Boyette's expression tightened at that. "Questions based on hearsay and old paperwork? Doesn't mean much."

"We're just trying to understand his role," Marcus said. "He left abruptly. No public explanation. And the timing raises concerns."

Boyette folded his arms. "People leave jobs. Life moves on. Doesn't mean there's some grand mystery behind it."

Lacy stepped forward. "Then it should be easy to clear up. We're only asking to review any public case logs he was assigned to."

The sheriff's smile thinned. "Miss Krammer, I suggest you don't go stirring up the past. This town has enough problems without ghosts being dragged out of closets."

"We're not dragging anything," Marcus said evenly. "We're trying to understand."

Boyette looked between them, then leaned in slightly. "Some things are better left where they lie. For your own good."

He turned and disappeared down the hall without another word.

Back outside, Lacy stood motionless. "He's hiding something."

"Probably more than one thing," Marcus said, opening his notebook again. "And now we know for sure—whatever this is, they don't want it found."

They had just stepped off the curb when a figure approached them from across the street.

"Miss Krammer. Marcus."

Lacy turned, tension flaring across her shoulders.

Dale Brower—the County Council Chair and owner of the feed store—strode across the narrow street toward them, his bolo tie neatly centered, a folder tucked beneath one arm. He moved with a practiced, public ease, the kind that made her skin crawl.

"I heard you were back," Brower said, his voice low enough not to carry. "Lot of folks have."

She held his gaze. "I'm not exactly hiding."

Brower didn't smile. "And yet you're asking questions most people have the sense to leave alone."

Lacy crossed her arms. "You mean questions about my grandfather's death? Or why someone's been lurking around his house?"

His jaw ticked. "I mean questions that stir up bad blood. The kind this county worked hard to bury."

"I'm not trying to stir up anything," she said. "I'm looking for the truth."

Brower stepped closer. "Then maybe you should ask yourself what you're really hoping to find. Sometimes the truth doesn't fix anything. It just burns what's left."

Marcus moved to her side, his posture calm but ready.

"Is that a threat?" Lacy asked.

Brower's mouth twitched. "It's advice. From someone who's been here long enough to know how quickly things can turn."

He turned and walked back to his truck, the door slamming shut behind him.

Lacy stood frozen a beat longer. Her pulse thudded in her neck, not from fear—but from recognition. That wasn't just a warning. It was a message. One meant for someone stepping outside the lines.

Marcus didn't speak until Brower's truck had pulled out and disappeared down the road.

"They're scared," he said to her. "You don't threaten someone unless you think they're close to something."

Lacy nodded slowly, the morning heat pressing close around her.

"Then I guess we are."

The ride home was quiet, but her thoughts weren't. She kept replaying the encounter with Brower—the hard glint in his eyes, the way his words had curled like smoke beneath her skin.

By the time she'd turned onto the gravel drive, her jaw ached from clenching.

She cut the engine, grabbed her bag, and was halfway up the porch steps when she heard the phone begin to ring inside.

Lacy hurried with the key, the lock sticking a moment before giving way. She stepped into the farmhouse and dropped her bag by the door just as the phone rang a fourth time. Crossing to the kitchen, she snatched the receiver on the fifth ring.

"Hello?"

"Lacy, what on earth are you doing at the sheriff's office?"

The voice on the other end came fast and sharp. Margaret.

The question landed with the weight of both worry and accusation.

"I had some questions," Lacy replied, keeping her tone even. "Things that aren't adding up."

"Well, now everyone's talking. I just got off the phone with Gladys Rowe, and she said her nephew saw you walking out of there like you owned the place. What are you trying to prove?"

Lacy closed her eyes and lowered herself into the worn armchair by the window. "I'm trying to understand why Grandpa died. Why there are footprints outside the house at night. Why someone tried to break in. Doesn't that matter to you?"

"Someone tried to break in," Margaret's voice cracked. "Who?"

"I don't know."

Margaret's voice softened. "This is Dry Creek, Lacy. People don't like things being dragged into the light."

"That's not a good enough reason to stop looking," Lacy said.

There was a pause, filled only by the faint buzz of the phone line.

"You don't know what you're dealing with," Margaret said finally. "There are people in this town who'd do just about anything to keep the past buried."

"I'm not looking to dig up dirt just to cause a scandal."

"But you might cause one anyway."

Lacy glanced out the window at the field beyond the fence,

the grass swaying like it knew something she didn't.

"Just be careful," Margaret continued. "You're not the only one folks are watching now. And once the town turns cold on you…" Her voice trailed off, and Lacy filled in the silence with memories—of clipped conversations in general store aisles, of polite smiles that ended too quickly.

"Thanks for calling," Lacy said after a beat. "I'll keep my head down."

As she hung up, her jaw tightened.

She hadn't come back to Dry Creek to keep her head down.

That evening, the farmhouse held the day's heat like a clenched fist. Lacy moved through the kitchen slowly, setting out plates and silverware with more care than necessary. The tension hadn't lifted. If anything, it had rooted itself even deeper since Margaret's call.

Marcus arrived just before dusk, his knock sharp but familiar. She let him in without a word and gestured toward the table, already set for two.

Neither of them had much appetite, but they picked at the food anyway—sautéed vegetables, rice, and a pair of too-dry chicken breasts. Conversation flickered between long silences.

"They're closing ranks," Marcus said finally, pushing a green bean to the edge of his plate. "Even the ones who aren't part of whatever this is—they're scared."

Lacy nodded. "Margaret's scared too. Her call wasn't just about gossip. She knows something—maybe not all of it, but enough to warn me off."

"Same with Brower. That wasn't just some power trip. That was damage control."

She looked out the window, where the last of the light was turning the field to ash. "George saw it too. Whatever he found, whatever he was putting together—it spooked them. Badly."

"We need a system," Marcus said. "To stay ahead. If something happens—if we lose contact—there needs to be a protocol."

She met his eyes. "Code words?"

He nodded. "And regular check-ins. Morning and night. We'll document everything digitally, back up the files in separate locations. If they're watching, we make sure they don't get a chance to erase what we've learned."

Lacy leaned back in her chair, absorbing the weight of that. The fear hadn't disappeared. But it had changed shape—into something sharper now. Cleaner.

She extended a hand across the table. "Deal?"

Marcus took it. "Deal."

Night had fully settled by the time Marcus stepped out onto the porch. Lacy lingered at the door, watching as his taillights disappeared into the dark.

She didn't go back inside right away.

The stars were out, brittle against the sky. A breeze rattled the hedgerow. Across the field, at the edge of the gravel road, a pair of headlights appeared—too far away for her to see the vehicle clearly. But they weren't moving.

They idled for a full minute. Maybe longer.

Then, slowly, they turned and disappeared into the night.

Lacy stood frozen, hand still on the porch rail.

The message was clear.

They were being watched.

And warned.

She went back inside, locked the doors and windows again, and sat at the kitchen table with her phone in hand, thumb hovering over the "call" button.

It buzzed before she could press it.

Unknown number.

She answered.

A long pause.

Then a whisper:

"Last chance."

The line went dead.

The silence that followed was worse than the voice itself.

Lacy lowered the phone slowly, its weight suddenly immense in her hand. Her pulse thrummed at the base of her throat.

She rose and crossed to the front window, lifting the corner of the curtain just enough to scan the darkened yard.

Nothing moved. No headlights. No sound.

But she no longer felt alone.

Chapter 8

The knock came early—firm and fast, as if the sender didn't want to give her time to hesitate.

Lacy opened the front door to find Marcus on the porch, a travel mug in one hand and a manila folder tucked beneath his arm. His expression was sharp with purpose but softened when their eyes met.

"Morning," he said. "Figured we should get a head start."

Lacy stepped aside to let him in. "You always knock like the house is on fire?"

"Only when it might be."

The tension from the night before still hadn't fully left her chest. That whisper clung to the back of her mind: *Last chance.* She'd slept in fits that night, waking at every creak and shift of wind.

Marcus moved straight to the kitchen table, spreading the folder's contents out across the worn surface—printouts, handwritten notes, and highlighted timelines.

Lacy joined him, rubbing at the sleep still clinging to her eyes. "Coffee's still hot. Help yourself."

He nodded but didn't move for the pot.

She pulled out a chair and sat. "Alright. Let's lay it all out.

What do we actually have?"

Marcus leaned over the table, finger tapping a folded page. "We have George's envelope—copies of town meeting minutes, budget reports, police reports, and letters. Some personal, some official."

She nodded. "Plus the names he marked in the margins. Cross-referenced with what we know now—people who died, disappeared, or were quietly run out of town."

He added a few newspaper clippings to the pile, each one dated years apart but disturbingly similar: unexplained deaths, obituaries with vague causes, accidents that seemed too neat. "Different decades. Same language."

Lacy picked up a list George had started—names in one column and dates in another, some circled in red. "This one keeps bothering me. My uncle Carl is on here. Margaret said he died by suicide back in the nineties, but…"

"…but his name shows up in the same year as another missing persons report," Marcus finished. "And both reports were signed off by the same deputy: Tolbert."

Lacy's mouth tightened. "If it was just one or two cases, maybe. But this many? Spread out like this?"

"Patterns don't lie. People do."

She looked up at him, the morning light edging through the window behind her. "You think George knew? That he was getting close?"

Marcus nodded slowly. "I think he knew more than he wrote down. And someone else knew he was digging."

Lacy exhaled, slow and steady. "Then we need more than just notes. We need proof."

He leaned back in the chair, folding his arms. "Time to take this beyond the farmhouse. We need records. Archives.

Something they didn't get to."

Her pulse ticked faster. She knew where he meant.

"Monroe County Library," she said.

"Exactly. You up for a field trip?"

She stood, brushing crumbs from the table. "Let me grab my bag."

Before they left, she gathered the loose papers from the table, tucking them carefully back into the manila envelope. Crossing to the china cabinet, careful not to rush, she opened the hidden compartment and placed the envelope back inside it. Only when the panel clicked back into place did she let out a slow breath.

Whatever had started with George's envelope—it wasn't buried yet.

The drive to Madisonville took just over forty minutes, Marcus's sedan hugging the curves of the county road as fields of soy and corn gave way to stretches of pine.

Lacy watched the landscape blur past from the passenger seat, her fingers absently drumming the edge of her notebook. Neither of them said much for the first leg of the trip, each turning over the same gnawing thoughts.

The County Library's brick façade finally came into view, nestled between a hardware store and a faded diner at the edge of town. Marcus pulled into a gravel lot and shut off the engine.

Inside, the air was cool and still, greeting them like a familiar ghost. A woman in her sixties sat behind the main desk, her eyes sharp above silver-rimmed glasses. Her name tag read "Ruth Gentry."

"We're looking for archived county records," Marcus said. "Dry Creek, mostly. Incidents from the late nineties and early 2000s."

Ruth studied them for a moment, then pointed down a

hallway. "Back room. Microfiche and paper indexes. Sign in first."

They jotted their names in the logbook and made their way through the dim rows of shelving. The archive room was hushed, lit by a pair of overhead fluorescents that hummed faintly.

Lacy settled at the microfiche viewer while Marcus pulled a labeled box from a shelf. They fell into a rhythm—reading, flagging, and quietly sharing anything that didn't sit right.

Half an hour in, Marcus tapped a clipping near the top of a manila folder. "Here."

She leaned over. A small column from 1997: "Thomas Greeley, age twenty-two, missing. Last seen near Route 7. Believed to have left town voluntarily."

"That's one of George's names."

Marcus nodded. "Now look at this—two months later, there's a death notice for Michael Hayes. Same street. No investigation mentioned."

"And no one connects the dots."

"Except us."

They exchanged a look. The room felt smaller now. Closer.

"Keep digging," Lacy said. "We're not done yet."

Lacy slid the next fiche into place and turned the dial until the blurred text came into focus. The headline read: *LOCAL GIRL RUNAWAY? FAMILY LEFT WITH QUESTIONS.* The photo beneath it was grainy, but the name—*Jenna Ralston*—leapt out like a slap.

"Marcus," she said, voice low. "She's on the list."

He leaned in as she adjusted the zoom. The article was from 2004. Jenna, sixteen, had vanished after school one Friday. Her backpack was found in a drainage ditch two days later. No signs of foul play, authorities had concluded. No search extended past the week.

"They ruled it a runaway," Lacy murmured. "But listen to this: the deputy quoted is Tolbert again. He says she 'was likely reacting to recent disciplinary issues at home.'"

Marcus frowned. "That sounds like they wanted it closed before it even opened."

She scrolled further down the article. In the comments from Jenna's parents, something stuck in her throat.

"Her mother said Jenna had anxiety but never talked about leaving. That she'd been scared of something. Someone."

Marcus was quiet for a beat, then stepped away and pulled another box from the shelf. "This is becoming a pattern."

Lacy followed him. "Young, vulnerable, and conveniently written off. Every time, Tolbert's name is on it. And then, shortly after… he's gone too."

"Transferred. Resigned. Vanished into retirement," Marcus said, rifling through more folders. "Whatever excuse they gave."

A thin binder near the bottom of the box caught his eye. He flipped it open, revealing a handwritten timeline—decades of incident dates paired with scribbled initials. No official stamp. Just careful pen strokes and a pattern too sharp to be coincidental.

"This had to be someone's personal record," he muttered. "Maybe another clerk, or a journalist. Look at this—1991, 1997, 2001, 2005… all have red X's next to them."

"And every one of those years lines up with one of the names in George's envelope," Lacy said.

Her pulse quickened. The room felt colder, the overhead lights humming louder somehow. She leaned back, the weight of what they were uncovering pressing in hard.

"Someone was tracking this long before George," Marcus

said.

"Then maybe someone else knew," Lacy replied, voice tight. "And maybe they didn't live long enough to say anything."

They stared at the binder, neither of them reaching for it right away.

Outside the archive room, the library remained quiet, distant laughter echoing faintly through the front stacks. But here, surrounded by the musty breath of history and paper, everything felt dangerous.

Lacy met Marcus's gaze. "We take photos. Of everything."

He nodded.

She glanced toward the exit. "Before someone decides this record goes missing too."

They stepped out into the late afternoon glare, blinking as the sunlight sliced across the library's gravel lot. The sky had turned a muted pewter gray, the kind of color that made it hard to tell whether a storm was coming or the day had just grown tired of itself.

Lacy tugged her jacket tighter as they crossed to Marcus's sedan. The notes they'd made were in a manila envelope tucked beneath her arm. Its weight didn't seem proportional to the danger it now carried.

"Let's head back to the farmhouse," she said.

Marcus nodded and reached for the keys in his jacket pocket.

That's when Lacy saw the car.

Parked just across the lot in the shadow of the diner—a black SUV, engine idling, front windows tinted too dark for legal standards. She hadn't seen it there when they'd pulled in. She would've remembered.

"Marcus," she murmured, stepping closer. "Don't look right away, but there's a car watching us."

His hand paused on the door handle. "Where?"

"Across from the hardware store. Driver's side facing us."

He opened the car door like nothing was wrong, tossing his jacket inside and lowering his voice. "Get in. Slowly."

They climbed in, doors clicking shut, the envelope placed carefully between them like fragile glass. Marcus started the engine and backed out, keeping his eyes on the mirror.

The SUV didn't move.

Lacy held her breath until they'd turned out onto the main road.

But two blocks down at the next intersection, the SUV pulled out and followed.

"They're not even trying to be subtle," Marcus muttered, tightening his grip on the wheel.

"Could be a coincidence," Lacy offered, though she didn't believe it.

"Not after everything we just found."

He took a left instead of heading straight back toward Dry Creek, looping through a residential area lined with ranch houses and gravel drives. The SUV still followed, keeping a few car lengths back.

A quick turn into a grocery store lot, weaving through the rows.

The SUV lingered at the entrance, engine idling.

Then it peeled off, turning down the side street without signaling.

Marcus exhaled. "You get a plate?"

Lacy shook her head. "Too much glare. But I got the make— GMC, newer model."

"Great," he said, pulling out again. "That narrows it down to about a million."

The drive back to the farmhouse was quieter than before, every bump in the road magnified by adrenaline. Lacy kept checking the side mirror, but the SUV never reappeared.

Still, the silence felt watched.

"Someone knows we're digging," she finally said, her voice low. "That wasn't a warning. That was surveillance."

Marcus didn't answer right away. "Then we start thinking like targets," he said at last. "No more leaving anything at the house. We make copies, keep them separate."

She nodded, gripping the envelope tighter. "Agreed."

As the gravel drive came into view, the farmhouse waiting like a question at the top of the hill, Lacy's pulse climbed again.

She didn't know what she expected—but she knew better than to expect safety.

Inside the farmhouse, the kettle let out a low hiss as Lacy poured boiling water over a pair of tea bags. Chamomile, something grounding. The envelope of copied documents sat on the counter, still damp around the edges from her grip.

Marcus stood near the back door, arms folded, his gaze drawn toward the treeline. "We need to keep a backup off-site. A thumb drive at my place, maybe another with someone we trust."

"Who do we trust?" Lacy asked, handing him one of the mugs.

He hesitated. "No one local. Not yet."

She sank into a chair at the table, the tea warm between her hands. "Feels like we're up against a wall of shadows. Every time we learn something, it gets darker."

Marcus joined her, sipping quietly. "Then we move in pairs. Keep phones charged. Schedule check-ins."

Lacy nodded. "Code word?"

He half-smiled. "Make it something weird."

She thought for a moment. "'Toothpick.'"

Marcus blinked. "Seriously?"

"It's unassuming. No one's going to guess that means 'I'm safe.'"

He chuckled once, the sound easing the tension for a flicker of a second. "Alright. 'Toothpick' it is."

They both fell quiet, the stillness between them not quite empty—more like an agreement settling in.

Outside, the wind stirred again, rattling the shutters softly. The sky had darkened, the first hints of dusk beginning to settle.

Marcus finished his tea and set the mug down. "I'll drive the long way home. Make sure no one's still tailing."

Lacy stood with him, walking him to the front door. "You'll text when you're home."

She watched his taillights vanish down the drive before locking up. Then she returned to the kitchen, double-checking the envelope from the library, her movements careful.

The sky had darkened to gunmetal, the air thick with the threat of rain.

She filled the kettle and set it on the burner. The click and low roar of the flame felt louder than usual; everything else hushed as storm-laden air pressed against the windows.

She made tea without thinking—chamomile again, out of habit—and stood sipping it by the sink. A gust shook the shutters.

That unease from earlier hadn't left. If anything, it had sharpened.

She set the mug down and went to the drawer, grabbing the flashlight.

Outside, the air had thickened, clouds rolling low over the

treetops. Lacy stepped out the back door, her boots landing soft in the damp grass.

The flashlight beam wavered, then locked onto something: footprints, sunk fresh into the earth.

She hadn't noticed them earlier. They hadn't been visible from the front of the house or the gravel drive.

She crouched. The prints followed the house, leading to the side yard, and disappeared beneath a window. There were no retreating footprints.

Her heart pounded. She rose fast, turned back for the house, and locked the door behind her with shaking fingers.

She crossed to the dining room, knelt by the china cabinet, and pressed the catch on the hidden compartment.

Empty.

The envelope, containing all the documents from George, was gone.

Chapter 9

Rain sheeted across the farmhouse windows, drumming a steady rhythm that had started before midnight and only deepened with each passing hour. The storm had grown teeth; wind clawed at the eaves, gutters overflowed, and the trees bent and groaned beneath invisible hands. Thunder cracked sharp and sudden, rattling the panes like a threat.

Lacy lay curled on the couch, blanket tucked around her shoulders, one hand resting on George's old shotgun propped against the coffee table. Sleep wouldn't come. Every time her eyes drifted closed, they snapped open again, the image returning to her: the hollow space in the china cabinet, the envelope gone.

She'd checked three times, as if disbelief alone could make it reappear.

On the end table, her tea sat untouched, gone cold hours ago. She reached for it out of habit, took a sip, then grimaced at the bitterness.

She leaned back, staring at the ceiling, counting the seconds between lightning and thunder. The gap was shortening.

And still, her thoughts circled back to the empty compartment.

Someone had been inside the house. While she and Marcus were at the library. Someone had walked into her home and taken the very thing George had died trying to protect.

She pulled the blanket tighter around her shoulders and lay back down, facing the darkened window, and somehow drifted into a restless sleep.

Gray light filtered through the curtains, muted and directionless. Lacy lay still, listening. The storm seemed to press against the house like a living thing—wind howling under the eaves, water gurgling in the gutters, branches tapping the roof in arrhythmic warning.

She sat up slowly, blanket falling to her lap. The air inside was cooler than it should've been. No hum from the refrigerator, no click from the heater. She glanced toward the kitchen and saw the digital clock on the stove—blank.

"Great," she muttered.

Power outage.

She swung her legs over the side of the couch. She hadn't gone upstairs the night before—hadn't wanted to be that far from the doors. Her mug of tea still sat half-full on the end table, cold and forgotten.

The rain had turned the world beyond the windows into a watercolor blur. The gravel drive had disappeared under sheets of water, and the trees bowed in the wind like penitents.

Lacy reached for the cordless phone and pressed the button. No tone. She tried again. Nothing.

She set it down more carefully than necessary and crossed to the front window. No signal bars on her cell. Not even a flicker.

A tightness pulled across her chest. "Okay. One thing at a time."

She tried the wall-mounted landline in the kitchen. Dead. Same with the one in the hallway by the pantry. Every line silent as stone.

She pressed her forehead to the cool glass of the window. No cars on the road, no movement anywhere. Just the endless surge of rain and the faint rattle of windborne grit against the siding.

Isolated.

Not just rural quiet—true isolation. No electricity, no landline phone, no cell service. And no way to know if Marcus had made it home or Margaret had heard a word of what was happening.

The farmhouse creaked under another gust of wind. Somewhere in the distance, thunder rolled long and low like a warning still too far away to be heeded.

Lacy stepped back from the window, crossing her arms to hold in the sudden chill. She'd always loved storms—how they cleaned the air and broke the heat, how they made the world feel small and close and alive.

But this storm didn't feel like that.

This storm felt like it wanted in.

She moved through the house with a growing unease, each step slower than the last. The thought had clawed at her all night: whoever had taken the envelope might've taken something else, too. Or left something behind.

She started in the front room, checking drawers, bookshelves, behind the couch. Everything looked undisturbed. The creaks in the floorboards sounded louder without electricity to mask them, each one echoing into the quiet.

In the kitchen, she opened the cabinets, pushing aside cereal boxes and a dusty cookie tin with nothing inside. The door to the basement remained bolted. Upstairs, the bedroom closet stood open, untouched. Nothing missing. Nothing out of place.

But she couldn't shake it. A wrongness lingered in the air— too still, too silent, as if the house itself were holding its breath.

Back downstairs, she crossed the front room without pausing, went straight to the china cabinet. Pulled the latch. Opened the hidden compartment.

Still empty.

The envelope she had returned there with care—replacing every page—was still gone.

The rain hadn't let up, but it had shifted—less wind-driven now and falling in steady, slanting sheets. Lacy stepped onto the back porch, ducking her head against the mist as she scanned the yard. Back in the house, the storm pulsed against the windows.

She stepped into the middle of the dining room, pulse tapping fast at her throat. The house moaned under another gust of wind, and her eyes flicked to the window.

There was no going outside—not in this.

She turned in a slow circle, gaze drifting from the kitchen to the hallway, then upstairs. Somewhere in the house, she was sure there had to be a portable radio. George had always kept one around; he'd insisted on it. But she couldn't remember where it could be now.

She checked the kitchen drawers first—junk, mostly. Rubber bands, twist ties, an old bottle opener. The pantry held only food, a flashlight with corroded batteries, and a mouse trap.

She headed upstairs, scanning the shelves in the hallway. The linen closet gave her nothing but sheets and the faint smell of cedar. She crossed to the master bedroom, flicked the light switch out of habit—nothing—and began working through the closet.

A stack of old photo albums. Boxes of winter clothes. She crouched, pulled a few aside, and reached into the shadows near the back.

Her fingers brushed plastic.

She tugged, and there it was—a battered portable radio, the kind with a telescoping antenna and a worn knob for tuning. Dust clung to the edges, but it looked intact.

She brought it downstairs, heart ticking a little faster.

In the kitchen, she yanked open drawers until she found a full pack of D batteries wedged behind an old phone book. She tore them open, slid them into the radio with steady hands, and turned the dial.

Static. A burst of garbled voices. Then—

"...Monroe County Emergency Management is advising residents to stay off all roads. Several low-lying areas are under flood advisory. Power outages reported throughout the region..."

Her shoulders sagged.

The world was still out there. But she was on her own.

Lacy set the radio on the windowsill, its quiet crackle the only voice in the house. Arms crossed, she watched the rain fall sideways across the yard and felt the weight of waiting settle in her chest.

A lull settled in the afternoon; not exactly a calm, but more a thinning of the storm's fury. The rain lightened to a curtain of mist, wind no longer screaming but continuing to whisper through the eaves. The kind of pause that felt less like relief and more like the moment before a change.

Lacy stood at the kitchen window, the radio's low drone murmuring behind her. She had made a second cup of tea, though it too had long gone cold in her hands. Her eyes moved slowly across the yard. The trees beyond swayed in a heavy rhythm, water dripping from every leaf and branch.

Then—movement.

She blinked and leaned in, setting the mug down hard enough to splash. Something—or someone—was there.

Just past the barn, near the line where the yard gave way to open field, a figure moved between the trees. Not quick. Not purposeful. Just a presence, shifting in the gauzy rain, almost lost in the veils of mist.

She held her breath.

The figure stopped, as if sensing her gaze.

Her pulse thudded loud in her ears.

She stepped back instinctively, deeper into the kitchen, heart knocking hard against her ribs. The figure didn't move. Didn't raise a hand. Didn't call out.

And then—it turned. Slowly. Deliberately. A shadow becoming fainter, one step at a time, retreating toward the line of trees beyond the barn.

Had she imagined it? A shape caught between wind and rain? She didn't think so.

She locked the back door again, bolting it with fingers that trembled despite her efforts to stay steady. She scanned the yard once more, but it was empty now. As if no one had ever been there at all.

Except she'd seen it. Just long enough to know it wasn't her imagination.

Someone had come back. Not to break in—at least not yet— but to watch. To remind her she wasn't alone out here. Not really.

She picked up the shotgun and rested it near the table. Then she turned the radio up slightly—not to hear more, but to feel less alone in the silence between each gust of wind.

The storm had softened, but the threat hadn't.

It was still out there.

Waiting.

She moved room to room as dusk crept across the windows, checking every latch, every curtain, every blind. The flashlight beam sliced through the deepening shadows, jittery from her grip.

In the front room, she pushed the couch tight against the door—it wouldn't really work as a barricade, but the act of putting it there felt like control. She slid the shotgun closer, resting it across her lap as she settled into the chair facing the door.

The house groaned around her, settling against the storm. The radio whispered in the background, mostly static now.

Lacy hadn't eaten. Her stomach was too tight, wound up in the uncertainty of what the night might bring.

She tucked the blanket tighter around her and waited. A flicker of lightning lit the room in harsh relief. Her eyes burned from not blinking.

She waited.

Sometime after midnight, her chin dipped toward her chest. A crack of thunder jolted her upright.

And then—

A scrape.

Low. Drawn out. Just outside the door.

Her heart stuttered, breath caught.

She reached slowly for the shotgun.

Someone—or something—was on the porch.

Chapter 10

Thunder cracked again, a jagged whip across the sky that rattled the windows in their panes. Lacy jerked upright in the chair, heart thudding, her blanket sliding to the floor in a tangle. For a moment, she couldn't place what had pulled her from sleep—then came the sound again.

A long, scraping dragging noise across the porch.

She didn't breathe.

The shotgun was already propped against the table beside her. She reached for it with both hands, careful not to knock over the lamp. The storm outside had eased, but it hadn't stopped. Rain whispered against the windows in soft sheets and the wind still sighed beneath the eaves.

She moved to the side of the front window and pulled the curtain back a sliver, angling for a view without being seen. Her fingers gripped the shotgun tighter.

Lightning split the sky in a brilliant flash—and for an instant, the entire porch was illuminated in silver light.

A raccoon stood by the tipped-over trash can, its fur soaked, its beady eyes wide and startled. It froze, then bolted across the porch and into the hedgerow.

Lacy let the curtain fall shut and pressed the back of her

hand to her mouth. A sound escaped her—not quite a laugh, not quite a sob.

Just a raccoon.

She lowered the shotgun and sat back down in the chair, adrenaline still churning through her veins. Her body ached from tension, and the weight of the sleepless night settled back into her bones.

She stared at the door.

Even if it hadn't been a person this time, it could've been. And that truth—the randomness of it, the way fear had crept in and settled like mold in the corners of her mind—stayed.

Eventually, she picked up the blanket from the floor and wrapped it back around her shoulders. The storm rolled on outside, quieter now but no less oppressive.

And still, she didn't sleep.

At first light the next morning, Lacy stood on the porch, the shotgun no longer in hand but also not far from reach. The storm had finally crawled east, leaving behind a sky the color of tin and air that smelled like wet soil and pine. The road beyond the gate was a patchwork of puddles and gravel, rutted where the runoff had carved shallow channels into the surface.

She rubbed at the grit in her eyes and checked her phone again—still no bars. Her last text to Marcus hadn't gone through, but she tried one more time anyway, thumbs tapping stiffly.

Can you meet me at Mitchell Yates' place? He's on the list. I think we've missed something.

She hit "send" and watched it spin, uncertain whether it would land.

The name had surfaced during one of their late-night sessions with the documents: Mitchell Yates, a retired county maintenance supervisor whose name kept appearing on old service requests near locations tied to several of the incidents. He was never directly listed in any of the summaries, but Lacy had felt the itch of something unfinished. Too many tangents circled him, none of which were connected yet.

She grabbed her bag from the front hall and slung it over her shoulder. The house felt stale behind her, like the aftermath of a fever. She didn't linger. She locked the door, paused long enough to slide the deadbolt, then headed for the truck.

The dirt lane was soft but passable, the truck's tires spinning slightly before catching. A curtain of mist hung low over the fields, turning every tree into a silhouette. Lacy tightened her grip on the wheel, the rumble of the engine her only companion.

By the time she pulled onto the county road near Yates' property, the mist had begun to lift. His weatherworn ranch sat hunched at the end of a gravel drive, the porch lined with wind chimes that clinked faintly in the breeze. A dented pickup was parked under a lean-to. No sign of Marcus yet.

She checked her phone again. Still nothing.

A shiver tightened her spine.

She cut the engine, stepped out, and stood there for a long moment, the wind tugging at her jacket hem. If she waited, she might lose the nerve.

Lacy adjusted the strap on her bag and started walking toward the front door.

One way or another, she needed answers. And if Mitchell Yates knew something, now was the time for her to find out.

She knocked twice on the door, firm but not aggressive, then stepped back. The porch groaned beneath her boots. No sound inside—no footsteps, no creak of movement. She glanced toward the truck under the lean-to. The hood was cool, windshield beaded with water.

Was he even home?

She knocked again. Louder this time.

Still nothing.

Her hand hovered near the doorframe, hesitating. Then she turned, meaning to head back to the truck and wait for Marcus.

The door opened behind her.

Lacy spun.

Mitchell Yates stood in the shadowed entry, a man in his late sixties with hollow cheeks and eyes set deep beneath a furrowed brow. He wore a flannel shirt, half-buttoned and stained with what looked like wood varnish. His expression was wary, not surprised. He didn't greet her.

"Mr. Yates?" she asked.

He didn't answer right away, his gaze flicking to the truck and then back to her. "You're Lacy Krammer."

It wasn't a question. Just a flat observation.

She nodded slowly. "I'd like to ask you a few questions, if you've got a minute."

He leaned one shoulder against the frame at that. "About what?"

"County maintenance records. From back when you were still working. Your name's come up on a few things I've been looking into."

His mouth pulled into a tight, unreadable line. "That was a long time ago."

"I know. But some of the places you were assigned to? They line up with other incidents. Deaths. Disappearances."

Still no change in his expression. If anything, he looked more tired than alarmed.

"Is there somewhere we could talk?" she asked.

"I've got work to do." He made no move to step aside. "If

you've got questions, ask 'em."

Lacy hesitated. "Do you remember a service call out near the old Meyers property? Fall of 2006. Road washout that was never filed with a follow-up?"

His eyes didn't move, but she saw something behind them stiffen.

"I remember it," he said.

"And?"

He glanced back over his shoulder into the house, then stepped partially onto the porch, pulling the door nearly closed behind him. "You want to be careful stirring up things that were already buried."

"I'm not trying to stir up trouble," she said. "But someone broke into my house last night. They stole a set of documents that might connect you to something bigger than a road washout."

His jaw twitched. "Then you really ought to stop poking around."

They stood in silence for a beat, wind sifting through the chimes like brittle breath.

Lacy took a small step back. "Thanks for your time."

Yates didn't reply. He turned, went back inside, and shut the door.

She stood there for a moment longer, pulse steady but sharp. Then turned to head back to the truck.

She never saw the figure moving toward her from the side yard.

The morning mist curled low along the edges of the house, wrapping the side yard in pale gray. Lacy's boots crunched lightly on gravel as she made her way toward the truck, hand already in her coat pocket fishing for the keys.

She didn't hear the footsteps—just the sudden shift of air behind her.

An arm clamped hard around her waist, another around her shoulders, wrenching her backward with brutal force. The world tilted. Her keys clattered to the ground.

She fought instantly—sharp, panicked, instinctive. Her elbow connected with something solid. She twisted, kicked, screamed. But a gloved hand caught her mouth, yanking her head back. Her scream came out muffled, barely more than a breathless grunt.

She bit down. Hard.

The grip faltered for a fraction of a second—just enough. She staggered free, stumbling toward the front of the truck, reaching for the handle—

A blow struck the side of her head. Stars exploded behind her eyes. She hit the ground hard, shoulder catching first, vision swimming. The gravel bit into her palms as she scrambled to get up.

A heavy knee landed on her back.

"No—" she gasped, her voice ripped raw.

She fought again—kicking, twisting, her breath coming in short, ragged bursts. But the weight was too much. A sharp jerk to her shoulder sent pain radiating down her arm.

Then something pressed to her face.

A cloth. Chemical. Sweet, cloying, wrong.

Her body recoiled, lungs begging for air that wouldn't come. Her limbs thrashed weakly, panic overriding everything. The edges of the world began to curl inward.

She heard her own heartbeat like thunder in her ears.

Then just the soft grind of tires over gravel—

And silence.

Sound returned first. Muffled. Distant. Like she was underwater.

The throb in her skull followed. Slow and mean, pulsing behind her eyes. Her mouth was dry, lips stuck together, the inside of her throat coated with something sour.

Lacy blinked once. Then again.

Darkness.

A dull, watery grayness filtered through a narrow seam beneath a door across from her. No windows. Just bare plank walls, a dirt floor scattered with old nails and straw, and the faint smell of oil and mildew.

She tried to sit up.

Couldn't.

Her hands were pinned behind her—tied, from the feel of it. Rope. Not too tight, but secure enough that her shoulders ached already. One of her boots had come loose and was now half off her foot. Her cheek rested against cold ground.

Panic surged, quick and bright. She gritted her teeth against it.

Don't scream. Don't move too fast. Take stock.

She inhaled slowly through her nose and tested her ankles. Not bound. Not yet. Whoever had dragged her here hadn't bothered.

That told her something. She just didn't know what yet.

A breeze whispered through a warped board overhead, and the groan of a tree limb answered somewhere outside. The shed—or whatever this was—stood alone. No footsteps. No voices. Just the settling creak of the structure and the sound of wind threading the rafters.

She rolled to her side, the motion awkward, her head spinning from the effort.

Who?

Why?

She tried to remember every detail before the world had gone black. Yates turning away. The mist. The moment she'd reached for the truck door.

A shadow moving.

Her stomach turned.

If this was connected to the missing documents—and it had to be—then someone had been following her. Maybe since the farmhouse. Maybe longer.

She leaned her head back against the wall and closed her eyes for a heartbeat.

This wasn't random.

And it wasn't over.

The quiet pressed in.

Lacy shifted again, testing the give in the rope around her wrists. It held. Her muscles were beginning to cramp, the ache climbing into her shoulders and neck. The cold had seeped into her jeans, into the soles of her feet. Damp earth, stale air. No windows. No way to track time.

She took another breath, shallow and slow, and strained to hear—anything.

Wind stirred outside. Distant. And something else—a low, rhythmic creak, like a tree swaying against another structure. No engines. No voices. No signs of life beyond her own heartbeat thudding in her ears.

She studied the space again.

The shed—if it was a shed—was maybe ten by ten feet with unfinished walls. No tools. No shelves. Just the faint scent of mildew, and something older beneath it. Rust, maybe. Or mold. Her stomach twisted.

Lacy tested her balance, bracing her knees and shifting her weight. If she could get upright—if she could—

She rolled to her side again, this time pushing with her elbows, working her boot against the floor. Her shoulder screamed in protest, but the movement gave her a little leverage.

Not enough.

She slumped back down, breathing hard. Her face burned with effort and frustration.

The questions returned, sharper now.

Had Yates set her up? Had someone followed her from the farmhouse? From the courthouse? And if so—what had they seen? What did they think she knew?

She hadn't told anyone where she was going—not even Marcus, not clearly. Just a half-delivered text. No reception. No witness.

Her throat dried again.

Think.

Someone had gone to a lot of trouble to disappear her. Not kill—at least not yet. That had to mean something. They needed something. Or they were waiting for someone else.

She twisted her wrists again, gently this time, feeling the texture of the rope.

No zip ties. Natural fiber. Scratchy. Coarse.

That was good. Maybe.

Maybe not.

Something creaked again—closer this time. Her breath caught.

Then silence.

Her pulse thundered.

She waited.

Waited.

Then—

The faint crunch of footsteps outside.

And the jingle of keys.

Chapter 11

The footsteps stopped just outside the door.

Lacy didn't breathe. Her heart thumped in her throat, loud and insistent. The jingle of keys stilled, replaced by the sound of a hand on the latch.

One second stretched into five.

Then the door creaked open.

Light spilled into the shed in a narrow band. A figure stepped inside, filling the frame. Broad-shouldered. Hooded. The lower half of his face covered with a dirt-smeared cloth. He ducked to clear the doorframe, and the moment he entered, the door thudded shut behind him.

He carried a length of metal pipe in one gloved hand.

"You don't know when to stop," he said, voice muffled but cold. "Should've stayed in your lane. But you couldn't leave it alone."

Lacy didn't answer. Her legs had gone numb hours ago, but her hands had more slack in the rope now—not much, but enough. She shifted subtly, fingers testing the knot again.

"You start digging," he continued, pacing slowly inside the shed, "and people like you always think the truth's going to help something. But it doesn't. All it does is drag up the rot and spread it around."

His voice was low, intimate. Measured. He crouched beside her, the pipe resting across his knee.

"You were warned," he said.

Lacy lifted her chin. "Yeah. I'm real bad at taking advice."

The man's eyes flicked with something like amusement. Or maybe pity. He reached toward her—just a flick of his hand, as if to check the bindings or maybe adjust her position.

She moved first.

Using the slack she'd earned, Lacy kicked upward with both legs, her boot catching him hard in the groin. He shouted—a raw, furious sound—and crumpled sideways, dropping the pipe as he doubled over.

She rolled, scrambling for the wall, but he caught her ankle, yanking her back. She twisted and kicked again, this time landing a heel into his ribs. He shouted again and let go, cursing, hands scrabbling for the dropped weapon.

Lacy dragged herself to the corner, heart jackhammering. Her arms burned from the strain, her wrists still tangled in rope. She pushed her back against the wall, ready to kick again.

But he didn't come closer.

The man staggered upright, breathing hard. One hand clutched the pipe; the other reached for the shed door. He yanked it open, stumbling out into the daylight. The door slammed behind him and she heard the latch click.

Locked.

Her breath came in gasps. Sweat slicked her neck and spine despite the cold.

He was gone.

But he'd be back.

Lacy leaned her forehead against the wall, forcing her breath to slow. The shed still reeked, but Lacy barely registered it now. Her senses were overwhelmed by the heat of her own breath and the cold grip of panic tightening behind her ribs.

The adrenaline hadn't faded. It coursed hot and sharp through her, sharper than the rope still cutting into her wrists. She turned her hands again, working the knots. They'd loosened more in the struggle, fibers stretched and warped from sweat and strain.

Come on, come on...

Her fingers were numb, but her focus narrowed to the one goal: get free before he came back.

The minutes stretched. She shifted awkwardly, managed to wedge her foot against a lower rung of the wall and used the leverage to brace herself. A tug, another twist, a flex of aching fingers—and suddenly, one wrist slipped free.

She gasped, half in shock, then reached for the other. It gave more easily, the remaining rope falling away in a tangle to the floor.

Free.

She didn't move at first. Just sat there, arms cradled to her chest, letting the tingling sensation rush back into her limbs like tiny needles. The skin at her wrists was raw, already beginning to swell in angry red bands.

But she couldn't stop now. She couldn't afford to wait for the next move to be his.

Lacy stood slowly. Her knees wobbled beneath her, muscles trembling from strain, but she stayed upright. The shed was as empty as before—bare rafters overhead, dirt floor underfoot, not a tool or spare board in sight.

She ran her fingers along the wall's interior, searching by touch. Rough boards, damp in places, cold to the touch. No hidden doors, no supplies. But maybe…

She crouched near the wall where she'd fallen earlier. One of the boards had felt soft under her weight—spongy, maybe loose. She tapped at it with the heel of her hand. It gave a little.

Just a little.

Her breath caught. If she could pry it loose—if she could find a weak point, or at least a slat to see through—maybe she'd get some sense of where she was. What was around her.

She needed a plan. She needed a weapon. She needed to get out.

Her fingers curled into fists.

The next time he opened that door, she wasn't going to be the one on the ground.

Marcus killed the engine.

Lacy's truck sat just off the road, just shy of the driveway. The windshield was fogged over. No one visible inside.

His eyes swept the lot, then the house.

He checked his phone again, the signal bar flickering in and out. Just one message had made it through: **Can you meet me at Mitchell Yates' place? He's on the list. I think we've missed something.**

No calls, no follow-up. Just that. Recent enough to matter. Recent enough to worry him.

Marcus exhaled through his nose and looked up at the house.

Mitchell Yates's place looked like it hadn't been painted in twenty years—gray clapboard siding sagging with age, a crooked porch rail, and one shutter barely clinging to its hinge. The windows were dark. Curtains drawn.

Marcus stepped out into the heavy morning air, the scent of wet pine and damp earth thick around him. He crossed the gravel slowly, boots crunching, pulse tight.

He didn't like this.

He climbed the porch and knocked once—loud enough to carry. Waited. Knocked again.

No answer.

He tried the door. Locked.

Marcus glanced around. No car in the drive, no movement in the windows. He stepped back off the porch and scanned the street. Nothing.

Across the road, a curtain twitched in a window. He walked across the grass and knocked at the neighbor's door.

After a long moment, an older man opened it, white T-shirt tucked into pajama pants, a frown already forming.

Marcus offered him a polite nod. "Sorry to bother you, sir. I'm looking for someone. Woman, mid-thirties, dark blonde hair, driving that pickup there. You seen her this morning?"

The man squinted past him. "She came by early. Knocked on Mitch's door. Didn't stay long."

"Anyone with her?"

"Not that I saw. But… there was a black truck pulled off down the road a little ways. Parked where the trees start. Not local. I don't think she saw it."

Marcus thanked him, then made his way back toward the road. The truck he mentioned was gone now. But tracks in the mud told part of the story.

His gut clenched.

Lacy had been here.

Now she wasn't.

And whoever had taken her had planned it.

He reached for his phone. No signal.

"Dammit, Lacy," he muttered, already heading back to his car.

He didn't know where they'd gone.

But he was going to find her.

Lacy searched the floor with her hands first. There were still a few nails scattered on the dirt floor, but none were sharp or long enough to be useful. No loose tools, no splinters strong enough to serve as a wedge. The rest of the shed yielded nothing of value. She moved cautiously now, steps soft on the dirt, ears attuned to any sound beyond the walls.

She crossed to the wall with the spongy board and dropped to her knees. The damp had softened the wood—not rotted it entirely, but enough to offer a weak point. She braced her fingers underneath the lowest edge and tugged, but it barely moved.

Her eyes swept the room again.

Then she saw it: a small metal bracket screwed into the far corner, maybe part of an old shelving mount. Barely more than a bent hook, but it caught the light just enough. She crawled over, picking up a nail from the ground and using it to pry the bracket free with a protesting squeal.

Back at the board, she dropped to her knees again and ran her hand along the base, fingers brushing the edge. A pair of old nails still pinned the bottom into place—half-rusted but holding firm.

She wedged the metal bracket beneath one of the nail heads and leaned her weight into it, careful but determined. The bracket bowed under the pressure, groaning as the nail resisted. She shifted angles, braced her boot against the floor for leverage, and pressed harder.

A crack split the air as the nail gave slightly—just enough.

She moved to the next one and did the same, and this time the board creaked inward a fraction of an inch.

Enough to get her fingers underneath it.

Lacy slipped them in carefully, breath caught, and pulled.

The wood resisted, then gave with another sharp snap.

She froze, chest heaving, heart pounding with the noise she hadn't meant to make. The echo of the cracking wood ricocheted off the walls, louder than it should have been.

Too loud.

Lacy froze, breath caught in her throat.

Outside remained quiet—but it was the kind of quiet that pressed in. No birdsong. No insects. Just the creak of trees in the breeze and the faint rustle of underbrush far off.

She pressed her ear to the seam in the wall, trying to listen for any footfalls, for the sound of boots over leaves or gravel or whatever terrain lay just beyond the planks. But all she heard was the rasp of her own breath.

One more pull. One more break might be all she needed.

She took a breath, braced again, and pulled.

The board split with a final, splintering crack that echoed like a gunshot.

Lacy flinched.

She let go of the board and scrambled back, heart hammering.

Silence again.

But it wouldn't last.

He'd heard that. Wherever he was—if he was nearby at all—he'd heard.

And now, he'd be coming.

Chapter 12

The sharp crack still echoed in her ears.

Lacy crouched in the dark, heart thudding, breath shallow as she strained to hear beyond the walls. The board she'd loosened now hung by splintered pieces of wood. Had he heard it? Was he coming?

Nothing. Not yet.

She forced herself to count to ten, then twenty, each number dragging through clenched teeth. No footsteps. No voice. Just the hush of wet woods beyond, soaked quiet like the world had stopped breathing.

She crept forward on her knees and reached for the board again. It hung loose where it had splintered, the bottom edge free. Just one more good pull would do it.

She gripped the dangling board, splinters biting into her palms, and gave it a sharp pull. It peeled away with a groan, swinging free. Damp air rushed in through the gap, cold and metallic in her lungs. She didn't hesitate.

The opening was just wide enough.

She crouched low and twisted sideways, one shoulder going through first, then the other. Her sweatshirt snagged on a splinter but she forced herself forward, hips squeezing through the tight space. She exhaled sharply and pushed off with her feet.

Her legs cleared with a jolt that left her sprawled on the wet grass.

For a moment, she lay still, blinking up at the pale slats of sky between the trees. The air smelled of rain and cedar and freedom. Her side throbbed where the boards had scraped her raw, but the pain didn't matter.

She rolled to her knees and ducked into the shadow of the shed, every sense sharpened. Nothing stirred in the clearing. No footsteps behind her.

She was out.

But she wasn't safe.

Rain dripped from the eaves and pattered across the ground. She scanned the clearing—tall grass, scattered rocks, trees thick with moss and brambles. About a hundred feet away sat a weathered cabin with a slumped roof and leaning porch, tucked deep in the woods. No signs of life. No smoke. No sound.

She moved.

Staying low, she crept into the underbrush. Each step was deliberate, every rustle of leaves a threat. She ducked into the tree line, bramble thorns tugging at her clothes, heart hammering.

Behind her, the shed stood quiet.

She slipped deeper into the trees, the wet earth soft beneath her boots.

Then—a sound.

The shed door creaked open.

The man stood in the threshold, silhouetted against the dim light, one hand on the latch and the other braced against the frame. His weight shifted—still favoring his leg she'd struck. For a second, he just stared into the dark interior.

Then he cursed.

The word cracked through the air like a shot.

He stepped inside, boots grinding against the floor. A pause. Punctured by another curse, sharper this time. The realization was sinking in.

She was gone.

Lacy crouched deeper into the underbrush, chest heaving silently. Through a narrow slit between ferns, she watched him stumble back out, whip his head toward the trees, and stagger toward the cabin.

He disappeared inside.

Seconds ticked past.

She fought to stay still, fought the urge to run while she still had the lead. Her whole body hummed with urgency, but her training screamed louder: *Wait. Watch.*

Then he reemerged—this time with a rifle.

She didn't need to see its full shape to recognize the outline. Long barrel. Wood stock. Heavy. He moved with purpose now, dragging a coat over one shoulder as he limped down the cabin steps and headed toward the tree line.

Toward her.

Lacy sprang into motion.

Not upright—she couldn't afford to be seen—but hunched low, weaving between trees and brush, feet sinking in soft moss and slick leaves. Every branch seemed too loud underfoot. Every breath scraped her throat raw. She pushed through a tangle of thorns, one catching her cheek and drawing blood, but she didn't slow.

Behind her, a voice rang out—sharp and furious.

"LACY!"

She didn't look back.

The forest closed around her, deeper and darker, the ground

rising uneven beneath her. She didn't know where she was going. She only knew she had to stay ahead.

She angled downslope, instinct guiding her toward denser cover where the trees leaned in tighter and the brush thickened. Her breath came fast now, throat dry despite the damp air, legs burning from the effort. Branches slapped at her arms, wet leaves smearing across her face like paint. The sounds behind her—footsteps, curses, twigs snapping—rose and fell unpredictably.

He was gaining.

She forced herself to slow—not stop, just slow—and listen. The ground here was soft, the rain having soaked deep into the layers of moss and old pine needles. If she could hear him, maybe she could estimate distance. Direction.

A crack of brush somewhere uphill. Closer than she'd hoped.

She pivoted sharply and dropped low, ducking beneath a fallen log. Her back scraped bark as she slid through the narrow space beneath it, teeth clenched to keep from gasping. On the other side, she scrambled into a shallow ravine cut by decades of rain runoff—its edges slick, walls soft with mud.

Her foot slid out from under her and she dropped to one knee, catching herself with a hand against the damp ground. The cold bit through her jeans. A sharp pain flared in her ankle but didn't hold. She pushed forward, half-crawling, half-dragging herself along the bottom of the gully.

Above, the woods were quieter now. The shouts had stopped.

Her heart pounded. She crouched low beneath the shelter of a jutting rock and pressed her fingers into the wet earth, steadying her breath.

Think.

He would guess she'd gone downhill—but maybe not this far. Maybe he thought she'd veered left. Her prints would be hard to follow on the muddy slope, especially in the undergrowth. She had to use that.

Doubling back was a risk.

But so was staying here.

She climbed out of the ravine, keeping her head low. The slope was steep, and her legs trembled as she fought for footing. She paused at the top, scanned the area. Still no movement.

Then she heard it again—him—farther off now, crashing through the underbrush, shouting her name. He'd gone the wrong way.

A tremble passed through her—not fear this time, but something closer to hope.

She turned east, angling toward higher ground, weaving through trees thick with lichen and vines. Her hands stung from cuts and her knees ached from crawling, but her focus narrowed to each step, each breath.

Every second she stayed free was a second closer to escape.

Or rescue.

If it came.

She pressed forward, keeping to the trees, searching for anything she could use—anything that offered cover, high ground, or even just a place to stop and think. The incline rose gradually and she followed it, stepping carefully over roots and weaving through brush thick with wet leaves.

Minutes passed—ten? Fifteen? It was hard to tell. Her body was shaking now, not just from the cold but also from the effort of keeping herself controlled, focused. At last, she reached a small rise where the forest grew dense and tangled, the canopy closing in tighter overhead. A tangle of fallen branches and overgrown underbrush formed a natural hollow just beneath a leaning cedar.

She dropped to her knees and crawled inside.

It was tight, the ground cold and littered with needles, but dry enough to huddle beneath and well-concealed from any angle unless someone were standing right over it. She curled into herself, back pressed to the cedar's base, and tried to slow her breathing.

Somewhere in the distance, a branch cracked. Then another. Fainter now.

He was still out there searching.

She pulled her arms close to her chest and forced herself to stay still. Her jeans were soaked, her sweatshirt clinging to her like a second skin. Scratches crisscrossed her hands and neck, a deeper sting along her ribs where she'd scraped the board getting out of the shed. But she was alive.

For now.

The underbrush rustled again, but farther west this time. His footsteps were uneven—still favoring that leg—but they were moving, relentless. She listened, barely breathing, as they moved. Farther. Then silence.

Only then did she allow herself a breath. Not relief—she wasn't safe yet. But distance was something.

And then—through the hush, a new sound.

Faint. Far off. But unmistakable.

An engine.

Lacy stiffened, pulse surging. It could be anything—a hunter, a local, someone coming up the old trail. Or—

Or him. A backup plan. Another threat.

She shifted slightly, readying herself. Whatever was coming, she needed to see it before it saw her.

And if it wasn't help, she'd be ready to run again.

Chapter 13

Lacy crouched in the thicket, damp leaves clinging to her sleeves, heart pounding against her ribs like it wanted out. The sound of the engine was closer now—low, guttural, and uneven, like a truck struggling through mud. Her breath caught as she strained to listen, each passing second twisting her gut tighter.

The thorns scraped her palms as she shifted to a better position, careful not to rustle the undergrowth. She didn't dare move too much. She had no line of sight from here—just the steady rumble growing louder, then leveling off. Whoever it was, they weren't barreling through. They were taking their time.

She tried to steady her breathing, but the air felt too thin. Was it him? Had he gone for help?

Lacy pressed her back against the base of a tree, biting down the rising wave of nausea. The engine groaned again, closer now—maybe thirty yards? Twenty? Her brain scrambled through the possibilities: a hunter, a lost hiker, a forest ranger. Marcus?

Please let it be Marcus.

Then, just as suddenly as it had risen, the sound began to fade. The vehicle didn't stop. It kept going. Down the trail, deeper into the woods, maybe veering off toward another turn.

She exhaled hard, shoulders sagging. Relief came sharp and sour—like she'd bitten into something half-rotten. It hadn't been him. And it hadn't been help.

The woods swallowed the sound, leaving only the faint rustle of breeze in the canopy and her own shaky breath. She was still alone. Still hunted. And now she knew: someone else was out here.

Lacy wiped the sweat from her brow, the damp chill of her skin grounding her.

Time was bleeding away.

She had to move.

Marcus gripped the steering wheel of his sedan a little tighter as he turned onto the narrow gravel spur branching off the main road. The rain had mostly passed, but puddles still dotted the track, and the occasional slap of wet leaves brushed the windshield. His tires crunched steadily over packed earth and gravel—slick in places, but nothing his car couldn't handle.

His phone rested in the center console, screen dark but not off. He'd gotten one message. Just one:

Can you meet me at Mitchell Yates' place? He's on the list. I think we've missed something.

No follow-up. No ping. Service had blinked in and out like a dying candle. Whatever tower had let that message through was probably miles back now.

Marcus's gaze swept the roadside. Trees hemmed him in on both sides—thick pine and maple, their wet branches drooping low. It wasn't the kind of place you stumbled across. You had to know where you were going.

Then he spotted them—fresh tire tracks veering off the gravel onto a narrower path. He slowed, letting the car idle forward. The tracks were deeper than his, thicker tread—definitely a truck or something heavier. Recent, too. The rain hadn't washed them out.

He eased the sedan onto the path, branches whispering along the sides as the forest pressed close. Around a bend, the trees thinned just enough for him to see it: a low, sagging cabin tucked back in the clearing, its porch slouched to one side and the roof streaked with age.

Marcus stopped the car, engine running. No movement in the windows. But something about the place prickled at him.

He reached over and flipped the glove box open, pulling out his flashlight. Then, after a second's hesitation, he reached down and tapped his holstered firearm under his jacket.

Just in case.

He continued forward until the car was nearly at the edge of the clearing, close enough to make a fast exit if he needed to.

Then he killed the engine.

And listened.

Lacy stopped, crouched lower in the thicket, every muscle trembling with the strain of staying still. The air around her hung damp and still, thick with the rot of wet leaves and the distant tang of woodsmoke—faint, maybe imaginary. Her legs had gone numb beneath her, but she didn't dare shift.

A twig snapped.

Close.

Lacy's breath hitched. The sound hadn't come from an animal. She knew the rhythm of footsteps—two slow paces, then a pause. Then again. Deliberate. Heavy.

She wasn't alone.

Her captor was near.

Panic fluttered at the edges of her control, but she crushed it down hard. *Don't run. Don't panic. Think.*

She angled her head slowly, listening for more. Another step. Closer now—ten yards? Less?

Lacy's training kicked in like a breaker being thrown. She sank further into the undergrowth, inching sideways on her elbows. The wet earth sucked at her sleeves. Thorns tugged at her shirt. She didn't care. Every movement was a calculation: *Shift weight here, press low, breathe shallow.*

A branch cracked behind her.

He was close enough to see her if she moved too fast. He continued.

She needed to disappear.

Instead of fleeing straight downhill, she twisted her path in a tight arc, following the slope upward. Higher ground meant visibility—riskier, but with better options. The brush thickened, branches clawing at her like grasping fingers. Still she climbed, slow and steady, silent as she could manage.

Halfway up the rise, she spotted a patch of ferns broken by an old game trail, barely a rut in the hillside but clear enough for her to slip into without too much noise. She followed it ten yards more then ducked behind a fallen log, heart in her throat.

She listened.

Breathing hard now, not from exertion but from the raw edge of adrenaline scraping through her.

The footsteps had stopped.

So had the woods.

Even the birds were silent.

Lacy pressed her back to the cold bark of a log and waited, every cell wired for movement. Her hand closed around a thick branch beside her—rough, solid, not too heavy. She kept it close, just in case.

Below her, a figure moved through the trees.

Closer than she thought.

Too close.

Marcus stepped out of the car slowly, boots sinking slightly into the soft, mossy earth. He scanned the clearing once more, eyes narrowing on the sagging porch and warped door of the cabin. A curtain hung in one window—no breeze. Just a limp, stained scrap, unmoving. The place was silent.

He moved forward, every footstep measured. Gravel gave way to patchy grass and wet pine needles.

The porch groaned under his weight as he stepped up. He tested the doorknob—unlocked. It gave way easily, the door swinging inward with a reluctant creak.

The interior was worse than the outside. Stale air hit him first—carrying the scent of unwashed clothes, old food, something faintly metallic. A single bulb dangled from the ceiling, unlit. Dust swirled in the weak light filtering through a high, cracked window.

He moved slowly, keeping low, flashlight sweeping across warped floorboards and cluttered furniture. Dishes in the sink. A moldy coat slumped over a chair. No sign of Lacy. No sound of life.

Then he saw it: a door at the end of the narrow hall, slightly ajar.

Marcus approached. The smell changed—stronger here. Something sharp and acrid beneath the rot. He pushed the door open with his foot.

The room beyond was different. Cleaner, somehow—but colder.

The walls were covered in papers. Newspaper clippings. Polaroids. Handwritten notes. Yellowed maps. It looked like a conspiracy theorist's bunker.

His flashlight beam paused on a photo—blurry but familiar. A shot of Lacy, taken from a distance. Another beside it: a group of local officials at a ribbon-cutting. And yet another—Marcus himself.

What the hell is this?

He stepped closer. The scrawl beneath the photos made no sense—fragments of sentences, numbers circled and underlined. "They don't see it." "Too late now." "Redemption through exposure."

There were dates. Some recent. A calendar marked with cryptic symbols. And in the center of the wall—a large photo of a woman with red hair, face scratched out in heavy black ink.

Marcus's stomach turned.

This wasn't just obsession.

It was a shrine.

He backed out of the room slowly, senses blaring. Whatever this was, it wasn't random. It wasn't harmless.

And Lacy was somewhere out there—alone with the person who'd built it.

Lacy crouched beneath the bramble edge, her breath shallow, pulse drumming in her ears. She had minutes—maybe seconds—before he circled closer. If she kept running blind, she'd run out of ground or luck. Or both.

Her eyes swept the terrain. The trail she'd followed curved downward into a narrow dip—muddy from runoff, slick with fallen leaves. Deer tracks dotted the edge. A game trail.

And a chance.

She crawled toward it, knees catching on vines, fingers numb. Her hand closed around a branch—solid, gnarled, maybe two feet long. Not enough to stop him, but enough to hurt. She held onto it as she surveyed the slope. A slick patch dipped near the trail's curve. Just below it, a line of low brush arched over the path, thinned by weather.

Perfect.

She knelt and began working quickly, dragging another limb into place across the incline. Wet leaves camouflaged her movements. Her plan wasn't to trap him completely—just to slow him, disorient him, buy herself an opening.

With the thick branch in hand, she dug out a wedge in the mud, half-sinking it in, then broke twigs and scattered bramble over the disturbed spot. Her hands stung with scrapes and cold, but she kept moving. She shifted a few stones, making the area look undisturbed. The rain had helped; everything was just damp enough to blend.

When she stepped back to look at her work, the trap was nearly invisible.

She turned sharply and angled around a cluster of trees, taking a wide loop that brought her back uphill. From this new vantage point, crouched between two boulders slick with moss, she could see both the trail and her makeshift trap.

The branch she'd claimed as a weapon rested across her knees. Her chest rose and fell in shallow bursts. She didn't feel brave. She felt wired, raw. But she wasn't going to wait to be found again. If he came this way—and she was nearly certain he would—she'd be ready.

A sound in the underbrush.

Twigs cracking. A grunt. Leaves whispering beneath boots.

Closer.

She steadied her grip on the branch.

Any second now.

A heavy footfall snapped a branch along the lower trail. Then another. Slower this time, with a hitch—like someone favoring a leg.

He was limping.

Lacy's eyes stayed locked on the trap below. The seconds stretched, taut and terrible. Rain ticked off the leaves above her, steady now. So was her heartbeat.

Another step. Then a curse. Muffled. Familiar.

She recognized his voice.

He didn't see the trap. Not until it was too late.

One more step and his foot sank where she'd buried the branch. He slipped—exactly where the slope turned greasy with runoff—and went down hard with a yelp, body twisting as he hit the mud and skidded sideways.

Leaves exploded upward. His rifle flew from his grip, landing in the muck halfway between him and her.

Lacy didn't think.

She launched herself from the rocks, crashing downhill in a blur of motion. Her feet skidded but she kept her balance, branch clenched tight. Her mind emptied—no words, just instinct and momentum and the raw, stinging drive to end this.

He rolled over, eyes wide. Scrambled to reach for the gun.

Too late.

Lacy swung the branch with both hands, catching him square in the shoulder. The thud of impact jolted her arms, sent a shudder through her spine. He grunted, lost his footing again, arm flailing.

The rifle slid farther down the slope.

They both turned at once—eyes locking on the weapon.

Mud-slick. Feet away.

For one breathless moment, they were frozen.

Then they each lunged.

Chapter 14

Lacy lunged.

Mud splashed up her legs as she propelled herself forward, the world narrowing to the glint of steel just ahead. Her captor hit the slope at the same time, arms flailing as he scrambled for the rifle, fingers inches from the stock.

She dove, hands outstretched, snatching a handful of wet leaves before finally feeling cold metal in her grasp. His hand clamped over hers a beat later.

They struggled in the muck—grunting, breathless, feral. The rifle slipped between them like a bar of soap. He drove a shoulder into her side, trying to shove her off. She twisted, brought her knee up sharply into his ribs. A bark of pain. He rolled sideways but kept hold of the barrel.

Her training surged to the surface—movements rehearsed in sweat and grit long before she'd ever set foot in this forest. She shifted her weight, pinning his arm beneath her hip, and yanked the rifle hard. The butt cracked against his chin, stunning him just long enough for her to wrench it free.

He roared and surged up, fingers clawing for her throat. She scrambled back, rifle now in both hands, her breath ragged and shallow.

"Don't," she gasped.

But he didn't stop.

She didn't have time to think—only to react.

His body launched forward again, and her finger found the trigger.

The rifle kicked against her shoulder with a thunderous crack.

He jerked mid-lunge, his shout collapsing into a strangled howl as he hit the ground hard. One hand clutched his shoulder, the other clawed at the muddy earth beneath him. Blood spilled between his fingers, bright against the gray-brown sludge.

Lacy stood frozen, the rifle still aimed, arms locked. Her ears rang from the blast, and her breath came in sharp bursts.

He writhed, groaning curses, trying and failing to sit upright. "You—" he rasped. "You don't know what you've done."

"I know exactly what I've done," she said, voice low, steady despite the tremble building in her knees. "And I'll do it again if you move."

The pain must've overtaken his bluster; his limbs sagged, his eyes squinting against the rain. "It wasn't supposed to be like this," he muttered.

She didn't answer.

Steam rose from the rifle barrel. Her hands, numb just moments ago, were suddenly aware of every cold rivet and edge of metal. Her arms ached, her side throbbed from where he'd driven into her, but she didn't lower the weapon. Couldn't.

Somewhere, a crow called once, sharp and distant.

Then, through the ringing in her ears, she heard something else.

Footsteps. Distant—but coming.

Marcus.

The name rose in her mind before she could believe it. She

tightened her grip anyway, unsure—praying.

Through the trees, a shape emerged, boots crunching through wet underbrush. A figure moved with purpose, cautious but quick. Then the face cleared the gloom.

"Lacy—"

Her knees almost gave out.

He stopped at the top of the incline, pistol in hand, eyes locking on hers, then dropping to the rifle in her hands. Then to the man sprawled at her feet.

"You're hurt," Marcus said, stepping forward slowly.

"I'm okay," she said, though she wasn't sure if that was true. Her hands were trembling now, the adrenaline ebbing and leaving something cold in its place. "He's not. Shoulder. He tried to—" Her voice cracked, and she swallowed it down. "He's down."

Marcus holstered his pistol as he crouched beside the man, rifle still aimed from Lacy's position.

"Sheriff Boyette," Marcus said under his breath, studying the blood-soaked fabric, the groaning man beneath it. "He's lucky you didn't shoot to kill."

"I aimed to stop him," she said. "That's all I could do."

Marcus met her eyes again, quiet approval emerging behind the concern. "You did more than most could've."

He reached for his belt, unthreading the leather with practiced efficiency. "We need to bind him before he decides to get brave again."

Lacy gave a single nod, stepping in just enough to keep the rifle steady. Boyette flinched as Marcus rolled him to his side and secured his wrists tightly behind his back.

The forest seemed to hold its breath with them—no wind, no birdsong, just the rhythmic rasp of Boyette's breathing.

"You're safe now," Marcus said.

But Lacy didn't answer. Not yet. Not until the weight in her chest lifted.

Not until she was sure this was over.

Marcus stood and gave the bindings one last check before stepping back. Boyette groaned, listing sideways in the dirt, blood soaking the front of his shirt, but the fight had gone out of him.

Lacy kept the rifle aimed. Her breath had steadied some, but the tremble hadn't left her limbs. "He said it wasn't supposed to be like this."

Marcus glanced up. "He say anything else?"

"Just that I didn't know what I'd done." Her brow furrowed, gaze fixed on Boyette's slack face. "I think he really believes that. Like this was something… righteous."

Marcus's jaw tightened. "That tracks with the rest of what I found."

She shot him a sharp look. "What do you mean?"

"I'll explain. But first we need to get back to the cabin. You're soaked and half-frozen, and we need to get a signal out."

She hesitated. Her boots were heavy with mud, her jeans soaked through. Every bruise, every scrape was making itself known now that the adrenaline had ebbed. She didn't want to move. But they had to.

Marcus touched her elbow. "Come on."

Together, they got Boyette to his feet—barely. He sagged between them, spitting curses through gritted teeth, one arm limp from the bullet wound.

They half-dragged, half-walked him back through the trees. Lacy stayed silent, eyes scanning the woods, waiting for something else to go wrong.

But nothing did.

As they reached the clearing's edge, the slumped shape of the cabin came into view. Peeling paint flaked from the siding. Lacy had never been so glad to see something so ugly.

Marcus nudged the door open with his shoulder and helped Boyette to the floor inside. The sheriff slumped back against the wall with a groan, blood seeping onto the warped planks.

Lacy stepped back, still holding the rifle. Her hands felt raw now. Splintered. She looked down at them like they belonged to someone else.

"I'll find a phone," Marcus said, already moving toward the back of the cabin. "Stay with him. Just in case."

She didn't respond; she just nodded, eyes never leaving the man on the floor.

Boyette smiled—just barely.

"You don't get it," he slurred. "None of you do."

Lacy raised the rifle an inch higher. "You're not talking your way out of this."

He coughed, then laughed, thin and bitter. "Was never trying to."

She stood her ground, knees locked, throat tight.

Whatever he meant, it didn't matter. Not now.

What mattered was keeping him right there where she could see him.

What mattered was the sound of Marcus's footsteps in the next room—and the hope that, just maybe, help was on the other end of the line.

The phone's brittle ring cracked the silence.

Marcus's voice followed—clear, urgent. "Yes, this is Special Agent Marcus Trent with the Tennessee Bureau of Investigation. We need emergency services. One injured suspect in custody. And a victim who's been through hell."

Lacy exhaled, just once.

The rifle was still in her hands, but for the first time in hours, she now allowed herself to believe she might not need it much longer.

Marcus returned from the back room, his expression tight but calm. Lacy stood where she was, rifle held loose but ready.

She didn't look at Boyette. She looked at Marcus.

"Special Agent?" she said, voice brittle. "That what I heard?"

Marcus nodded slowly. "Yeah."

"You're not a freelancer."

"I am a freelancer," he said. "But not the kind I let people think. I was embedded here by the TBI. Investigating Monroe County corruption—missing persons, unusual deaths, complaints that vanished. Sheriff Boyette's name kept coming up."

Lacy took a step back, the weight of the rifle pressing against her palms. "And me? I was part of the investigation?"

"You were never part of it," Marcus said quickly. "But your grandfather's death flagged something in the system. That's what put you on my radar. I didn't know what you were chasing until you started pulling at the same threads I was."

Her eyes didn't leave his. "So everything you told me…"

"I meant it," he said. "Every word. But I couldn't tell you more without risking the case—or your safety. I needed to know who I could trust."

She let the silence stretch between them, heavy and hard.

Finally, she exhaled. "I get it. Doesn't mean I like it."

"No. And you don't have to. Just know this—I never lied about what matters."

Lacy looked away, blinking fast. Her voice came softer this time. "I knew something didn't add up. Guess I just didn't want to believe it."

Marcus stepped closer, voice low. "I'm here now. We're going to make sure he doesn't hurt anyone again."

She nodded once.

Then turned back toward the doorway, rifle still in hand, and resumed her place beside the man who'd tried to kill her.

Whatever she felt about Marcus Trent, TBI, or the lies between them—it would wait.

First came the reckoning.

Chapter 15

Sirens pierced the stillness of the woods, cutting through the hush like a blade. The sound grew louder, closer, until flashes of blue and red lit the trees beyond the clearing.

Lacy didn't lower the rifle until the first deputy stepped into view, voice calm but firm. "Ma'am, it's okay—we're law enforcement."

Her arms trembled as she slowly passed the weapon over, barrel pointed down. Mud streaked her sleeves, her fingers raw and bleeding, but her grip didn't falter until the deputy took the rifle from her hands.

Behind her, Boyette—the man who had held her captive—groaned on the ground, his shoulder slick with blood. Paramedics moved in swiftly, their voices clipped and professional as they began treating the wound. Another deputy read him his rights as Boyette continued to curse through clenched teeth.

A second cruiser pulled up, tires spitting gravel. More deputies fanned out across the clearing, some heading toward the cabin, others forming a wide perimeter. One deputy took Marcus aside, checking his ID and confirming his credentials. Lacy watched from where she stood, motionless, her breath catching as Marcus nodded and gestured toward her.

"Get her a blanket," someone said.

"Check her vitals."

Lacy barely registered the voices. Her ears rang from the rifle's report, and her knees threatened to give beneath her. But she stayed upright. Boyette was in custody. She was alive. And for the first time in hours, she didn't have to run.

A deputy guided Lacy gently toward the rear of an ambulance. She eased down, the blanket draped over her shoulders already soaked through from the damp in her clothes. Her muscles twitched from the adrenaline drain, her fingers stiff and red.

Someone handed her a bottle of water. She took it without speaking, twisted off the cap, and drank—mechanically at first, then in deep, grateful gulps.

Across the clearing, Marcus sat on the bumper of a cruiser, his shoulders slack, his face smudged with dirt and something darker. He glanced over, met her eyes. For a moment, nothing needed to be said.

A deputy stood beside her, notebook in hand. "Miss Krammer? I'm going to take a preliminary statement, just the basics for now. You can give us a full account once we're back at the station. Is that alright?"

Lacy nodded. Her voice cracked on the first attempt to speak, so she tried again. "Yeah. That's fine."

The prompts came gently, each one simple: her name, how long she'd been held, if she'd recognized the man, if she'd fired the weapon intentionally. She answered as best she could, her voice growing steadier with each response.

The interview didn't last long. Just enough to log the essentials while the memory was fresh. Across the clearing, Marcus finished his own round of questions, his expression unreadable. Another deputy stood nearby, jotting down notes, nodding occasionally.

The radio crackled with updates—ambulance en route to the hospital, perimeter secure, cabin cleared. The clearing pulsed with the activity of procedure, but it all felt strangely distant around Lacy, like she was sitting inside a snow globe that hadn't quite settled.

She glanced at Marcus again. He was already looking at her. When their eyes met this time, there was something quieter between them—something shared.

They were both still here. That mattered.

A deputy led Lacy to a cruiser, softly saying, "We'll take you both back to the station now. You can rest a bit on the way."

Lacy offered a faint nod as she got into the back seat, settling deep into the seat. Her legs ached, her joints stiff from the cold and adrenaline crash. She caught Marcus's eye as he approached another cruiser, his steps slow, the fight finally leaving his frame. A clean blanket had now replaced the one he'd had slung around his shoulders earlier, and his hands were red from scrubbing away dirt and blood at the paramedics' portable station.

Lacy watched Marcus's cruiser from the back seat of her own, her window fogged faintly from breath and damp. Trees slipped past, bare-limbed and gray against the fading light. The sun had dropped low over the hills, casting long shadows across the road. A hush had fallen in the car. The deputy driving didn't speak, and Lacy didn't try to fill the silence. She leaned her head against the cold glass and let herself feel the fatigue pressing in.

Her eyes drifted shut, just for a moment. When they opened again, the cruiser had reached the outskirts of Madisonville. The winding forest road gave way to pavement.

They pulled into the lot behind the Monroe County Sheriff's Office, where a pair of uniformed deputies waited by the door.

Marcus was already stepping out of his cruiser as Lacy climbed from hers. Their eyes met again.

"You good?" he asked quietly, voice scratchy.

She hesitated, then gave a small nod. "Getting there."

The building was warm inside, the lights too bright after the gray woods. A deputy led them through the side entrance and into a small break room, where someone had set out a stack of clean blankets and coffee thermoses. Lacy gratefully accepted both, wrapping the new blanket around her shoulders and cradling a hot cup between her palms.

"Undersheriff Minor'll want your full statements soon," the deputy told them. "Take a minute. You've earned it."

Lacy sat down beside Marcus on a bench along the wall. For a while, they didn't speak. Just breathed. Just sat still.

"You think it's over?" she asked at last, her voice barely above a whisper.

He looked straight ahead. "For him? Yeah. For the rest of it... maybe it's just starting."

Lacy didn't reply. But she didn't argue either.

The buzz of fluorescent lights hummed in the background, the warmth of the room seeping into her bones. She stared at her boots—still caked in mud—and felt the exhaustion begin to settle more fully.

A deputy stepped into the break room, holding a clipboard. "We're ready for you now," he said.

Lacy stood, her limbs reluctant but moving. Marcus rose beside her, and together they followed the deputy down a quiet hallway. Framed photos of past sheriffs lined the walls. The building smelled of strong coffee, disinfectant, and old paper.

They were shown into separate rooms. Lacy's was small but warm, with a padded chair and a fresh notepad laid out on the table. A female deputy offered her a refill on coffee and a soft smile.

"Take your time," she said.

Lacy nodded and settled in. Then the questions began.

She spoke slowly at first, the words heavy on her tongue. But as the details poured out—the shed, the cabin, the chase through the woods—her voice found a steady rhythm. The deputies listened without interruption, their pens moving steadily.

When she mentioned Boyette's connection to her grandfather, their expressions changed subtly—more alert, more focused. One deputy jotted something in the margin of his notepad and exchanged a glance with the other.

As the session wound down, one of them said, "We've already recovered a lot from the cabin. Files. Photos. Even some recordings. This could blow open more than just your case."

Lacy's hands tightened around her coffee cup. "What do you mean?"

"We think Boyette may be tied to other disappearances. Unsolved cases going back years. Some of it looks like it was personal. Some of it… maybe not. But your statement fills in some gaps."

A long silence followed.

Lacy blinked. "So that's it, then? It all comes out now?"

"It has to."

She let out a shaky breath. "Good."

And for the first time since it had begun, she believed it.

Marcus stepped into the hallway just as Lacy emerged from her interview room, blanket still draped around her shoulders, coffee cup half-empty in her hand. The fluorescent light overhead cast pale rings beneath her eyes, but her posture had straightened now, her steps more sure.

They met in the narrow corridor, neither speaking right away.

"You holding up?" Marcus asked, voice low.

Lacy nodded. "Yeah. You?"

He gave a tired half-smile. "Getting there."

A deputy passed behind them, murmuring into a radio. Somewhere farther down the hall, a phone rang and was quickly answered. The station hummed with quiet urgency, but here in the space between two doors, it felt like a lull.

Marcus motioned toward another empty bench just down the hall. "Come on. Let's sit a minute."

They sat down beside each other again, the air between them no longer thick with fear, but something more reflective. The silence held, comfortable this time.

After a long pause, Lacy asked, "You really think this'll bring closure? For the other families?"

Marcus looked at her, his expression gentler than she'd seen it all day. "I think it's the start. A lot of people have been waiting a long time to understand what happened to someone they loved. You gave them that."

"I didn't solve anything," she said, glancing down at the rim of her cup.

"You survived. And you fought back. That's more than most could do."

She let the words settle, unsure whether to feel comforted or overwhelmed.

A deputy walked past, nodded politely at them. Lacy watched him go, then turned back to Marcus. "Did they find anything else at the cabin?"

"A lot," he said. "Enough that this won't just get swept under the rug. I think Boyette kept trophies. Logs. Maps. He's been planning things for years."

Her stomach turned. "God."

"They're cataloging everything now. The TBI's already involved. I'm just glad it's over."

She was quiet for a beat. Then: "You're going to stay with the case?"

Marcus nodded. "At least until the handoff's complete. I owe you that much."

"You don't owe me anything."

He looked at her. "I do. If you hadn't made it out... none of this would've come to light."

Their eyes met again, the moment holding longer than before.

He stood, adjusting his jacket. "Come on. I think they've got a few more questions for me, then we're done for tonight."

Lacy rose beside him, slower this time. The fatigue was bone-deep now, but she followed.

Together, they walked down the hallway—two survivors stepping out of the worst of it, and into whatever came next.

Lacy stood at the sink in the women's restroom, hands braced on either side of the porcelain basin. The harsh fluorescent light buzzed overhead, reflecting off the scratched mirror in front of her. Her reflection stared back out at her—mud-streaked, pale, with shadows under her eyes and a faint bruise forming on her jaw. She barely recognized herself.

Slowly, she turned on the faucet. Cold water rushed out, biting against her scraped knuckles. She cupped her hands beneath the stream and splashed her face—once, then again. Mud and blood swirled in the basin, circling the drain. She watched it disappear, as if rinsing away the last hours would somehow make them easier to hold.

But it didn't. Not really.

She dried off with a coarse brown paper towel, then stared

at her reflection again. Her pulse had finally slowed, but the tremor in her hands remained. She tucked them under her arms, hugging herself as the chill returned.

There was no going back to the woman who'd arrived in Dry Creek looking for answers. That woman was gone. What remained was someone new—someone forged through survival, pain, and a fire she hadn't known she still carried.

A knock came at the door. "Lacy?" Marcus's voice, soft. "You decent?"

She cracked the door open. He stood on the other side, holding something small in his hand. "You left this," he said, offering her the locket—her grandfather's, the one she'd worn like armor since the day she'd arrived.

Her breath caught. She hadn't even realized it was missing.

"It was on the floor in the cabin," he said. "Figured you'd want it back."

She reached out, fingers brushing his as she took it. "Thanks."

Their eyes held for a long moment. He started to step back, then hesitated. "They've got him under guard at the hospital now," he said. "It's over, Lacy. You did what you had to."

She nodded, fingers closing tightly around the locket. "So did you."

They didn't hug, didn't need to. The quiet understanding between them said enough.

"Come on," he said. "Let's get out of here."

She followed him into the corridor, the hallway still lit by the same flickering lights but now feeling less sterile. Less suffocating.

As they reached the lobby, a deputy held the door for them. Outside, the last rays of sun bled through thinning clouds, streaking the sky in faded gold. The rain had passed. The storm had broken.

They stepped out into the evening together, side by side.

139

Chapter 16

The kitchen table was covered in paper—deeds, bank statements, utility records, all neatly stacked and secured with rubber bands. Lacy stood at the counter with a cup of coffee in her hand, her gaze unfocused. She'd been staring at the same page for ten minutes, the words swimming through her tired mind without meaning.

The farmhouse was quiet, just as it had always been in the early mornings. Dust motes drifted through slanted sunlight from the window above the sink. Outside, the pasture glistened with dew, the fences straight and solid just the way George had always kept them. He'd taken pride in the details: tight corners, freshly stained wood, weeds trimmed back every Sunday after church.

She set the mug down and moved to the table, sorting through the final stack of documents. The lawyer in Sweetwater had made it easy—too easy, really. Sign here, initial there, this one goes to the bank. But each signature felt like another thread cut. She was wrapping up a life, and there was something sacred in that.

Later, she walked the property slowly, boots damp from the grass, her fingers trailing along the fence posts. Every inch of this land held memory. The back gate where she'd once chased fireflies. The barn where George had taught her how to patch a tire. The big hickory tree where he used to sit and whistle, always off-key, always cheerful.

She paused at the edge of the pasture and looked back toward the house. The roofline was sagging a bit on the north end. She'd meant to fix that. The thought stung.

Somewhere behind her, a hawk called out, sharp and sudden. Lacy turned her face to the sky. The air was crisp with autumn now, the trees beginning to bronze along the ridges. She breathed deep and let the scent of pine and earth anchor her.

The porch steps creaked as she climbed them one last time. Inside, she opened the small wooden chest George had kept beneath the bench by the fireplace. Inside were letters she'd written from overseas, photos from her childhood summers, and a watch that hadn't worked since the late nineties but he'd kept anyway.

She held the watch in her palm, thumb brushing over the cracked face. "Thanks for waiting on me," she whispered.

Then she tucked it gently into her bag.

It wasn't just a house. It was the heart of something good. And she would carry that with her, wherever she went.

By the time she locked the front door behind her, the sun had crested fully above the ridge, painting the fields in gold. Dry Creek lay quiet in the valley beyond, but Lacy could already feel the shift—like the whole town was finally exhaling after a long, dark winter.

At the general store, folks no longer crossed the street when they saw her coming. There were nods toward her now. Gentle, uncertain smiles. Some even paused to speak—neighbors who hadn't said a word to her since George's funeral.

"Lacy," one older woman said, reaching out to squeeze her arm. "I'm so sorry for how folks treated you. We were scared. That's no excuse."

Lacy nodded, not trusting her voice. The apology felt raw and overdue, but honest. She'd come to Dry Creek expecting to leave with only a closed chapter. Instead, she'd found layers she'd never expected—grief, yes, but also grit and goodness.

At the café, the waitress brought her a piece of peach cobbler without asking. "From Mr. Ambrose," she said, setting it down with a shy glance. "He said to tell you… thank you. For standing up when nobody else would."

Lacy blinked down at the plate, warm and fragrant. She picked up her fork slowly, the weight of gratitude settling deeper than she'd expected it to. It wasn't validation she'd wanted—not exactly—but she felt something loosen in her chest all the same.

Outside, she passed the post office, where someone had tacked a photocopied article to the community bulletin board: **LOCAL HERO UNCOVERS DARK SECRETS IN MONROE COUNTY.** Her name was written there in bold, but she barely registered it. What mattered more were the pictures beneath—smiling faces of the women who'd gone missing, now finally acknowledged and mourned.

She stood there for a long moment, reading their names again. Letting them imprint on her.

A gust of wind stirred the paper, and she reached out instinctively to smooth it flat.

Behind her, someone honked—just once, quick and familiar.

Marcus pulled up, window rolled down and sunglasses pushed up into his hair. "You headed anywhere, or just haunting the square?"

She smiled, real and tired and unguarded. "Just saying

goodbye."

"Mind if I walk with you a minute?"

She nodded, and he parked along the curb.

Dry Creek had changed. Maybe not all at once. Maybe not enough. But the silence was broken now. The truth had aired. And people were looking at her—not with suspicion, but something closer to hope.

They walked the length of Main Street side by side, unhurried. The sidewalk was warm beneath the afternoon sun. Lacy kept her hands in her pockets, the silence between them comfortable for a while.

"So," she said finally, "you sticking around long?"

Marcus shook his head. "Another day or two. Paperwork mostly. I've got to debrief with the TBI office in Chattanooga." He glanced at her, gauging her mood. "And you?"

"Leaving tomorrow." Her voice was quiet. "Back to base, then… we'll see."

He nodded. "You did more here than some people manage in a lifetime."

"Don't romanticize it," she said, but there was no bite in it. "I nearly got myself killed. Twice."

He smiled faintly. "And yet here you are. Standing. Breathing."

They stopped near the town hall steps, where a few townsfolk lingered in quiet conversation. Lacy leaned against the wrought-iron railing, the sun catching in her hair. "I didn't come here to start something, Marcus. I just wanted to understand what happened to George."

"I know," he said. "But what you uncovered… it matters. A lot. You gave people a reason to talk again."

She looked over at him, skeptical. "And what about you?"

A beat passed. Then Marcus laughed, low and genuine. "I

don't know. Maybe I'll finally take a vacation without a cover story."

Lacy huffed a breath of dry amusement. "You should. You've earned it."

He reached into his jacket pocket and handed her a folded slip of paper. "My real number. In case you ever need anything."

She took it, tucking it into her wallet without looking. "Thanks."

They stood there a moment longer, watching as the town moved gently around them. A boy rode past on a bike, a dog barked at nothing in particular, and the air hummed with the ordinary sounds of life resuming.

"I meant what I said," Marcus added. "You're not alone in this."

"I know," she said, and for the first time in a week, she meant it.

Then she turned toward the town hall lawn, toward the path that would take her home one last time. Marcus fell into step beside her. Neither said another word.

They didn't need to.

At dawn, the sky turned a soft, watercolor gray—light bleeding slowly over the ridgelines like a promise. Lacy stood alone at the edge of the pasture, duffel bag slung over her shoulder and one hand wrapped around the strap like it anchored her to the moment. The farmhouse behind her was dark now, windows shuttered, the porch swept clean.

The airport shuttle idled near the mailbox at the bottom of the drive, engine low and steady. A young driver waited inside, respectfully not rushing her. She'd asked him for a moment, and he'd nodded without a word.

She let her gaze sweep over the property one last time. The

barn roof caught the morning light. A cardinal flicked through the branches of the hickory tree. Somewhere out near the treeline, a deer moved cautiously through the mist, barely visible.

This wasn't just George's land. It had been hers too, in laughter and scraped knees and whispered secrets. In every scarred fencepost and rusted hinge, there was also something of her.

She swallowed hard.

The screen door creaked behind her. Marcus stepped out, wearing the same dark jacket from the day before. "You sure you're ready?" he asked.

"No," she said honestly, but with a faint smile. "But I'm going anyway."

He nodded and offered her a thermos. "Coffee. It's awful. But it's hot."

She took it with a soft laugh. "Thanks."

They stood in the hush between words for a moment, just listening—to birds waking in the trees, to the engine humming down by the road, to the quiet creak of old wood under their feet.

"You'll come back?" Marcus asked finally, his voice low.

Lacy didn't answer right away. She looked at the farmhouse again, then out toward the hills. "Yeah," she said at last. "I think so. When my enlistment's up next year, it might be the right time to start a new chapter here. Finish the law degree, maybe hang a shingle."

"Good," he said. "Dry Creek needs more people like you."

She met his eyes, searching for something she couldn't name. "Take care of them. If you're still around."

"I will," he said.

Then she stepped off the porch and walked toward the

shuttle. The gravel crunched beneath her boots. Just before she reached the door, she turned back and lifted one hand in a small, steady wave.

Marcus raised his in return.

The shuttle door closed behind her with a soft hiss. A moment later, the van rolled down the lane, taillights glowing faintly through the fog.

And the farmhouse stood quiet again—watching, waiting, holding its memories close.

As they drove toward the airport, Lacy watched the landscape roll by—fog clinging low to the hills, barns half-lost in morning mist, and fields brushed gold by the rising sun. The shuttle ride had been quiet, the driver polite but silent, the road winding like a slow farewell through the heart of Monroe County.

At the terminal, everything moved with the soft hurry of a small-town morning. She checked her duffel bag at the counter and made her way through security. Her body ached from the past week—bruises blooming along her arms, muscles stiff from tension she hadn't let herself feel until now—but it was the ache in her chest that lingered most.

She settled into a plastic terminal seat and cradled the thermos Marcus had given her, now lukewarm but still grounding. Across from her, a child bounced in a seat, clutching a stuffed rabbit. A businessman spoke into a phone in clipped tones. Life moved on, indifferent and insistent.

Lacy stood when her flight was called, smoothing her jacket and adjusting her shoulder bag. As she walked down the jet bridge, her footsteps felt both heavy and light at the same time—as if every step she took away from Dry Creek was also a step moving her toward something else.

The plane was half-full. She took her seat by the window

and fastened her seatbelt, resting her forehead briefly against the cool glass. Outside, ground crew moved with quiet purpose, loading the last of the luggage.

Then the engines rumbled to life and the plane taxied forward.

As the wheels left the runway and the earth fell away beneath her, Lacy's breath caught—not in fear, but in awe. She saw the valley spread out below, a patchwork of fields and trees and winding roads. Somewhere in that green quilt was a house with a sagging roof. A pasture full of memory. A man she might see again, someday.

The clouds opened just enough to let sunlight pour through in long, golden rays.

Lacy leaned back in her seat, eyes half-closed, the corners of her mouth softening into the hint of a smile.

The past no longer held her. And the future, for the first time in a long time, felt wide open.

www.ingramcontent.com/pod-product-compliance
Lightning Source LLC
Chambersburg PA
CBHW021209130726
47988CB00002B/582